FINAL ADJOURNMENT

D1738236

A Washington Statehouse Mystery

Don Stuart

Epicenter Press

ᴡᴡᴡEpicenter Press

Epicenter Press is a regional press publishing nonfiction books about the arts, history, environment, and diverse cultures and lifestyles of Alaska and the Pacific Northwest.
For more information, visit www.EpicenterPress.com

Cover and interior design: Aubrey Anderson
Editor: W.P. Garrett and Aubrey Anderson

Cover Photo: Library of Congress, Prints & Photographs Division, photograph by Carol M. Highsmith, LC-HS503-858 (ONLINE) [P&P]

ISBN: 978-1-935347-78-1

Library of Congress Control Number: 2017941687

10 9 8 7 6 5 4 3 2 1

Contents

Prologue
An Unwelcome Breach of Decorum 1

Chapter One
Disrupted Plans 3

Chapter Two
Counter-Petition 8

Chapter Three
A Situational Assessment 15

Chapter Four
A Prime Sponsor 19

Chapter Five
Touching Base 28

Chapter Six
A Failed Motion 34

Chapter Seven
Unsolicited Support 37

Chapter Eight
Strategic Alliances 42

Chapter Nine
Parliamentary Inquiry 50

Chapter Ten
A Return to the Order of Business 60

Chapter Eleven
Reaching Out to an Ally 64

Chapter Twelve
A Strategic Sidebar 71

Chapter Thirteen
A Brief Recess 79

Chapter Fourteen
Old Business 88

Chapter Fifteen
Public Discourse 90

Chapter Sixteen
Temporary Accommodation Between Foes 94

Chapter Seventeen
An Off-Calendar Encounter 101

Chapter Eighteen
An Uneasy Collaboration 107

Chapter Nineteen
An Independent Witness 113

Chapter Twenty
The Loyal Constituency 118

Chapter Twenty-One
An Honorary Hiatus 121

Chapter Twenty-Two
A Gap in the Record 123

Chapter Twenty-Three
Dead Letter 129

Chapter Twenty-Four
Failed Motion of Censure 138

Chapter Twenty-Five
Vote on Final Passage 141

Chapter Twenty-Six
A Late Addition to the Agenda 144

Chapter Twenty-Seven
An Official Inquiry 157

Chapter Twenty-Eight
Suspension of the Rules 163

Chapter Twenty-Nine
Sine Die 174

About the Author 182

Prologue

Monday, March 1, 1:25 p.m.

An Unwelcome Breach of Decorum

I t was a scream to freeze time.

A dozen conversations came to a simultaneous halt as it echoed down the halls of the Irv Newhouse Senate Office Building. On the tree-lined walk outside, startled people stopped to look up through the branches toward the half-open second-floor window from which the scream had come. A passing tour guide broke off mid-sentence in his lecture to eight tourists. Two dozen noisy 6th graders visiting the Legislature on a social studies field trip were instantly silenced. A passing delegation of activist chefs professionally attired for their annual legislative "lobby day" went suddenly motionless—a stationary tableau of white caps and aprons.

Inside the building, lobbyists and constituents had begun to accumulate for their afternoon appointments. "What the hell was that?" said someone leaning out of a doorway at the far end of the second-floor hall.

"Guess somebody's bill died," joked her friend.

The scream had come from room 210, the office of State Senator Abel J. Mortenson of the 42nd Legislative District on Northern Puget Sound. Senator Mortenson was the long-time Chair of the Washington State Senate Committee on Natural Resources and a six-term fixture in Olympia.

"Maybe they finally stuck a knife in the old fart," said a dark-suited lobbyist waiting for an appointment in the office next door.

"Couldn't happen to a nicer guy," replied his companion. Nobody

1

else heard, but both men would later regret those comments.

An elderly Sergeant-at-Arms at a desk near the building's entrance was the first to act. He left his post and moved quickly but cautiously up the stairs. As he reached the second floor and proceeded down the long hall his look was stern. There were several people in the hall; all eyes were turned toward the far end of the building where sobs could be heard coming from an open door at the top of the back stairs. As he approached, the Sergeant-at-Arms looked carefully inside, then to his left in through the open interior door to the Senator's private office. Standing there, her hands on her face, crying uncontrollably, was the Senator's Legislative Assistant.

Seated inside, behind an immaculate oak desk, was the Senator himself. He leaned far back in his huge executive chair. His arms hung limp at his sides. His suit jacket was opened wide and he wore no tie. In the center of his perfectly starched white shirt was a large dark stain. And from the center of that stain protruded the intricately carved bone handle of an antique Native American hunting knife.

Chapter One

Monday, March 1, 3:00 p.m.

Disrupted Plans

As I stepped out through the front door of my home office on Water St., a Washington State Patrol car pulled up at the curb and two young uniformed officers came up my walk.

"Your name 'Torrence Dalton'?" one officer asked.

"Sandy Dalton, yes." My awkward first name, Torrence, is on the door, but everybody calls me Sandy.

"Mind if we step inside a moment, sir?" They were a couple of blond, clean-cut young men who, beneath their impressive uniforms, looked like they could be just out of college. Sensing my hesitation, the slightly older officer, Fitzroy according to his nameplate, added: "Won't keep you long."

Somehow, I knew this visit wasn't as routine as that implied. I was already late for a hearing. I'm a lobbyist, what the legal profession calls a "government relations specialist." I wanted to know what would be said about a bill coming up this afternoon. It wasn't that critical, however, and I didn't see how I could refuse, so I reopened the front door and invited them in. They younger one, Hughes, followed me back inside while Fitzroy stayed out on the front porch for a few moments and got on his phone.

We were apparently waiting for someone else to arrive.

My office is in a residential neighborhood, but the Newhouse Building, at the south edge of the State Capitol campus, is only a block and-a-half away. We don't get a lot of "walk-in" visitors, but Helen, my elderly admin, dutifully appeared and offered the two young officers "coffee or a coke," which made me smile. They declined and she slipped back into her office while the two policemen and I waited in silence.

After only a few minutes, through the front window I saw a tall, older, uniformed officer stride up the sidewalk and turn up my driveway. I stepped out and held the door open for him, feeling slightly intimidated. I'm a lawyer by training and I did some criminal work when I was a JAG officer the U.S. Navy, but I now specialize in government relations. I'm not accustomed to dealing with the police.

In my line of work, however, I understand how to deal with people in authority.

The senior officer was a Lieutenant Wilson who led some kind of "General Investigations Unit" in the Washington State Patrol. He was a good head taller than his two young colleagues, black with greying hair, totally serious, and obviously thoroughly competent and in charge; a distinct contrast to the two younger guys who were immediately deferential. I led them all into my conference room and, once we were seated and introduced, Wilson pulled a clear plastic document sleeve out of his briefcase and laid it on the table. It contained a single printed page.

"Recognize this?" he said, sliding it across in my direction.

"Yeah, I do," I said. "It's mine. I mean, I wrote it. Where did you get this?"

"You had an appointment with Senator Abel Mortenson at eleven-forty-five this morning?"

"Yes, I did. I left this with him. What's happened? What's this all about?"

"When did you leave the Senator's Office?"

"Noon, I guess. Maybe a few minutes after. Judith, his Legislative Assistant, had gone to lunch."

"Anybody else there?"

"Um… no, I don't think so. He keeps his lunch hour free. The House and Senate office buildings typically clear out during lunch."

I was thinking about the significance of these questions and of the interest in the document. On closer examination, I could see that it had a smear on it and splatters of what looked like blood. My pulse accelerated.

"Where have you been, Mr. Dalton, since you left Senator Mortenson's office at, as you say, 'a few minutes after noon'?"

"I walked back here. As you see, it's just down the street."

"Anybody else here? Can your secretary or someone here confirm your whereabouts over the past few hours?"

"Sure. Well, at least since about one or so. When I got back I believe Helen, my admin, had already stepped out for her lunch." I motioned toward the open door behind him. "She's here now. You can ask her. I also have an associate but she's been on the hill all day, won't get back till after five." Helen's desk was just the other side of the open conference room door. She knows everything that goes on in this office—a trait I both appreciate and rely on. In fact, I'd have bet that she was in there now, listening intently to every word we spoke.

"I see," he said.

From the sound of his voice, I wasn't sure he did. "You know," I said, "when I left the building, I went down the back stairs and out the rear entrance, the one that heads in this direction." The back of the Newhouse building was right on the edge of the Campus, just across the street from my residential community. "I believe there's a security camera there at the foot of the stairs…"

"Uh, huh," Wilson said. It wasn't really an answer. He looked around. "You live here?"

"Well, I do part of the time. I have a condo in Seattle. This is mostly just my business office. I'm single, so during Session I often stay here rather than make the commute."

"Were you at home in Seattle last night?"

"No, I was here. I drove down for a wedding yesterday and got back a bit late. I slept here last night." At the wedding, I'd run into a friend, Paula McPhee. Paula is an aide to Governor Carl Browne. She rents an older townhouse just a few blocks away from my office. It had been an especially nice Sunday afternoon and, after the wedding, I'd driven her and her daughter, Marissa, out to Priest Point Park for a little visit to the beach and then out to dinner. Afterward, we drove to Paula's place and, after she put Marissa to bed, Paula and I had stayed up awhile, talking.

Lieutenant Wilson just nodded. "Uh huh, and when you returned from your meeting with the Senator, did you change clothes?"

"No." I shook my head. "This is what I've been wearing all day. My jacket's there on the hook."

Wilson looked over at officer Hughes and made a slight head motion. The officer immediately walked over and carefully inspected my suit jacket.

Then, in a change of course, Wilson asked: "You mind explaining to me what this paper is all about?"

I was beginning to mind. My meeting with the Senator had been quite unpleasant; there's no getting around the fact that the man was an arrogant asshole. There'd been raised voices; very likely Judith had overheard. I was starting to wonder how much I ought to explain.

My lobbying practice specializes in natural resource issues. Among my clients are several commercial fishery trade associations, industry advocacy groups, and fish processing firms. Everyone who fishes, commercially or for sport, competes for a limited natural resource, particularly with salmon. Declining salmon runs and Northwest Indian fishing treaties are producing shorter seasons and tightening restrictions, especially on the non-Indian catch. This has created a political battle between the sport and commercial fisheries; some would say it's a fight over who gets to catch the last fish.

The controversy does keep my practice thriving with competing legislative bills nearly every session. But, for me, it isn't just about the business. I grew up in a commercial fishing family. This is stuff I was brought up to care about.

That document was the result of a battle over two of those bills.

I leaned back in my chair and looked across the conference table: "I understand, Lieutenant." I said. "You need some answers, but, so do I. This is going to take some explaining. Before I do all that, I'd appreciate you telling me what is going on here. Has something happened to Abel Mortenson?"

"Why would you ask that, Mr. Dalton?" Wilson replied.

The question was too pat and "innocent." I couldn't help but shake my head. I nodded toward the document on the table. "Well this looks very much to me like blood. The last time I saw this paper it was on Senator Mortenson's desk, and it sure as hell wasn't splattered with blood. You're asking me for my whereabouts. You want to know if I changed clothes in the middle of a work day and then you had your officer checking out my jacket. I'll tell you what, I'm happy to do everything I can to help you. But, as I'm sure you're aware, I've already answered several of your questions and you've answered none of mine. If you want me to help you, Lieutenant, first I think, you need to square up and tell me why you're here."

Clearly, Wilson didn't appreciate the challenge. He tensed up for a moment, but then he nodded and said: "Fair enough, Mr. Dalton. Senator Abel Mortenson was found in his office, at one-twenty-five this afternoon, stabbed to death. As far as we know, you're the last person who saw him before he died. According to his Legislative Assistant, you and he had a heated disagreement, parts of which she overheard before going out to lunch. Perhaps you'd like to tell us what that disagreement was all about?"

Chapter Two

Monday, March 1, 3:30 p.m.

Counter-Petition

I was momentarily stunned. I don't know exactly what I'd expected, but it certainly wasn't the Senator's death.

My initial thought was about the political impact. Senator Mortenson was a key figure in the Legislature. He was also Chair of one of my clients' key committees. His death was going to be big news. It would sure as hell alter my legislative strategy.

The more immediate reality, however, was that I was obviously a suspect. Should I ask to see a lawyer? Probably. I considered that, for a moment, but then decided "no." I'd done nothing wrong. Aside from attending a scheduled appointment at the critical time, I didn't see what there could be to implicate me?

What I said was: "Okay. I understand, Lieutenant. So, sure, here's what we argued about. Among other things, the Senator's on Rules Committee. He has influence. He's been holding up a bill that the Salmon Gillnet Association, one of my clients, needs if its members want to keep fishing."

"Okay. So that's it? You argued about a bill he didn't like?" Wilson smiled doubtfully.

"Well, actually, it was mostly the Senator arguing with me and there's a bit more to it."

"Uh huh. Naturally."

That didn't sound good. Fleetingly, I reconsidered my decision about the lawyer, but then I continued: "The bill allows the Department of Fish & Wildlife to authorize some specific, badly needed modifications to salmon gillnet fishing gear that will prevent federally protected migratory seabirds from getting tangled in the nets. All the State and Federal agencies agree. The environmentalists insist on it. If the gillnetters don't get it, their fishery could be shut down—we're talking tens of millions of dollars and several thousand lost jobs. The bill's a win-win. Clearly in the public interest. You'd think that would make it a slam-dunk, right?"

Lieutenant Wilson seemed to be tracking. The other two officers were saying nothing. One of them was staring out the window, the other seemed to be taking notes but from where I sat they looked like doodles.

"Well, at least it would have been," I went on. "Except, apparently, I pissed off the good Senator. So, he decided to bottle up my bill in Rules Committee. It had passed the Senator's Natural Resources Committee, no problem. With his support, I might add. Then I mentioned his name in a legislative update in the WCSC Newsletter—that's the Washington Commercial Salmon Coalition. Their newsletter gets a lot of circulation. Much of it is in the Senator's 42nd District. When he read my report, he started dumping all over our bill in Rules, where it's currently hung up."

"So, your fishermen friends will be happy to see Mortenson removed from the picture, right? Now you can get your bill back on track."

"Not really. But you were asking what this is," I said, pointing to the document on the table. "This is my article, the one he was so mad about. I printed it out on paper and took it with me today. I was hoping to calm him down. He'd built the thing up in his mind as a lot worse than it is. I wanted him to reread what I'd actually written."

Wilson spun the plastic sleeve around and took another look. "Okay, so that doesn't make sense to me. That's not what this article is even about. What you've got here is all about something entirely different, some kind of sports priority bill. What does that have to do with gillnets and birds?"

"Nothing, Lieutenant, and that's sort of the point. This other bill, HB 2343, is one that we're opposing. It prioritizes sport over commercial salmon harvests. It greatly restricts our catch and could badly damage our industry. It passed the House and is now in the Senate before Mortenson's Natural Resources Committee. Last week

Mortenson decided to give it a hearing later this week. We'd asked him not to do that. That's the bill I was writing about here in this newsletter article."

"Okay," said Wilson. "I get that Mortenson was maybe going to screw you over on this bill you didn't like. Right? But I still don't see what that has to do with the bird thing. What's the one got to do with the other?"

"That's the thing, Lieutenant. The two bills have nothing whatever to do with one another. They don't even involve the same fishing group. Only thing they have in common is that I'm the lobbyist on both. And, of course, that their fate is in the Senator's hands."

Wilson was obviously still confused.

I reached out and pointed to the printed sheet on the table in front of him. "Here," I said. "This is what I wrote. Read it and see what you think."

The article was very brief. It was on page two in a small font and hidden beneath a big display ad where it was quite inconspicuous – except that, in our meeting, Mortenson had circled it in red. When I'd first seen it in the e-newsletter, I'd been a bit miffed that the editor hadn't given it better play.

What it said was:

> HB 2343 (Sport Priority) passed the House and has been referred to Senate Natural Resources Committee chaired by Senator Abel Mortenson. Against our objections, Senator Mortenson scheduled a hearing for Thursday, March 4 at 3:30 p.m. in Senate Hearing Room #2 in the John A. Cherberg Building at the Capitol. Senator Mortenson may be undecided about this bill. We encourage everyone to come testify against the bill and to contact Senator Mortenson and other Members asking them to oppose this legislation.

Lieutenant Wilson looked it over: "This is it? This is what made him angry?"

"Doesn't seem like much, does it? I thought it was pretty gentle. I was peeved with him when I wrote that, but I wanted it to be tame because we still need... um, needed, Senator Mortenson's help. I thought I could convince him to stop that sport-priority bill in his Committee. He gave it a hearing, but he could still have voted against it himself or just refused to bring it up for a vote."

"So, you're telling me this little statement, here, this was why he bottled up your other bill, the one you need about the gillnets and birds?"

"Exactly. In other words: he was using the power of his public office to get personal payback against me for, apparently, making him look less than wonderful with some of his constituents. That seabird bill should pass. But Abel Mortenson was not what you might call a 'statesman.' "

"It certainly doesn't seem worth getting excited about. Just what did you do in that meeting that got him so upset?" Wilson asked.

"Not much. I may have pushed him a bit, but very gently. Mostly, I just listened. He'd plainly decided to be angry. I think he had to get that out of his system; needed a chance to berate me before settling down to make what we both knew was the reasonable decision."

"Still, it seems like you and your fishermen clients had a really big bone to pick with Senator Abel Mortenson. Both because he was maybe going along with these recreational fishermen on this sport priority thing and because he was holding up your other gillnet-birds bill, the one you seem to need so badly. You look like the last person to see him alive. When you did, the two of you had a heated argument. And to top it off, you'd apparently written some critical things about him. It doesn't sound like there was any love lost between the two of you. How'd he react to your 'gentle' pushing?"

"Not that well. I imagine Judith heard some of his more 'choice' responses from the other side of that door." I thought about that. "I bet she'll tell you that the angry voice she heard was the Senator's. Not mine." I was gratified to see him write down a note about that.

"So... what was he going to do about these two bills?"

"The thing is, Lieutenant, in the end, Abel Mortenson is a practical man. He's always been, I guess you'd say, high maintenance, but he came around."

"I'd think you'd want to keep on a friendly basis with the man."

"Absolutely. I did. I just carefully reminded him where his votes come from—and campaign contributions. I even offered to write a nice, supportive, laudatory piece about him in the next newsletter. In the end, I think he understood perfectly well. We parted on comfortable terms."

"And how about now? With him dead, will you get what you need now?"

"Well, with the Senator gone, I'm not really sure where my clients stand. Mortenson's death is going to throw a monkey wrench into things, that's for sure. I'm going to have some work to do over the next few days. But I think we still have the votes in Committee. I don't see it really changing much from my clients' point of view." I paused. "But then I guess you're asking about me personally. Right? "I had to smile. "For me, I guess it works out whatever happens. Over the years, I've learned that nothing in this place," I waved in the direction of the Capitol a couple of blocks away, "none of it is permanent. People come and go, even Abel Mortenson."

I wasn't entirely sure Wilson would immediately realize just how much Mortenson's absence was likely to affect the balance of power in Olympia. In real life, Mortenson was an elderly, semi-retired real estate broker from Bellingham, but here in Olympia, he was a powerful public figure. "I guess you know Mortenson has been caucusing with the Republicans?" I continued. "As a result, they've been, basically, running the Senate."

"Mortenson was a Democrat, right?"

"Yes, but once one of these people wins election and becomes a Member here, they can caucus and vote with whomever they want. Their constituents' only recourse is to kick them out in the next election. Just before this year's Session, Mortenson decided to join the Republican Caucus. His vote has put them in power. That affects a lot, including all the Committee Chairs. Now, with him gone, all that could change."

"I see."

"You know, Lieutenant, there are going to be a whole lot of influential people who will be happy to see him gone. And I'm, actually, not necessarily among them. Nor are my clients. He voted our way nearly every time."

"Wouldn't his voters think he'd betrayed them, doing something like that? Joining the other party?"

"Well, betrayal is one way to see it, and many definitely did. People also like a renegade. With a lot of voters, the Senator's 'independence' has just made him more popular. I do think the odds of that caucus arrangement hanging together over time, certainly past the next election, were pretty thin. When it fell apart, and it would have, Mortenson would have been left with a lot of very bitter enemies. Definitely including Democratic loyalists. My guess is that this Session with Natural Resources would have been his last committee chairmanship for a while, at least as a 'Democrat.' That's if he could have survived the coming primary. Of course, if he lost in the Democratic primary, he could still always just run as an Independent."

I could tell Wilson wasn't all that familiar with politics and the Legislature. "These fishery fights over catch definitely aren't the best way to manage declining salmon runs," I said. "Or to protect migratory birds, for that matter, but they do pay my rent. Senator Mortenson was one of the people that helped me stay successful at all this." That last bit may have been more cynical than I actually felt. I sure wasn't about to kill some Senator over a policy disagreement.

I was relieved when, a few minutes later, all three of the officers were in their patrol car headed back toward the Capitol. I wasn't entirely sure how my neighbors felt about me conducting business in their residential neighborhood, so I tried to keep a low profile. Nothing draws attention or makes a neighbor ask questions like a cop car parked in front of the house next door. I was also thankful I wasn't with them in that car on my way to some police interrogation room for further questioning.

Before they'd left, I'd let them briefly search my office and upstairs bedroom. Wilson also talked with Helen, apparently confirming that, even though she'd been out to lunch when I'd returned from the Capitol, as far as she could tell, I hadn't changed my clothes while she was gone.

There was one satisfying note. As the Lieutenant was leaving, I mentioned Clive Curtin's name as someone who might be worth asking about Abel Mortenson's death. Clive is a sport fishery leader who's responsible for a good deal of my commercial fishery clients' grief. A genuine pain in the ass. I told Wilson that Mortenson had been a much bigger thorn in the sportsmen's side than he'd ever been in ours.

Let "Clever Clive" answer a few of the Lieutenant's pointed questions.

Wilson was in the front passenger seat with his window down, shaking his head as the patrol car pulled away from the curb and rolled slowly down my narrow, tree-lined, residential street back toward the Newhouse Building and the Capital Campus.

I could tell the Lieutenant didn't much respect what I did for a living. In his book, maybe any lobbyist would be suspect. His work probably didn't call for a lot of diplomacy. He lived by the law. It was something for me to remember.

Some knowledgeable criminal attorney would probably have advised me to remain silent; to refuse to answer the Lieutenant's questions. There was, however, a very practical reason for cooperating. I'd wanted to clear this up as quickly and decisively as possible. To be publicly hauled in as a suspect, innocent or not, could end my lobbying practice. A lobbyist suspected of murdering a legislator would hardly be welcome in other legislator's offices. Few clients would be inclined to rely on his influence.

It's also possible, however, that I answered the Lieutenant's questions simply because I hate conflict.

It started in my childhood; my mom was big on "principle." When people behaved badly, as they so often do, she always had to let them know about it, clearly, very often loudly and in public. At times like that, I just wanted to disappear.

Given that history, it might seem surprising I became a lobbyist. Of course, when I first started, I was terrifically nervous that I might say the wrong thing or unwittingly offend someone. I just did what I'd always done in my lifelong effort to avoid conflict: consider the other person's point of view.

There are always clues. They often aren't subtle. If you walked into a Republican legislator's office, for example, and saw a huge American flag covering nearly an entire wall and an antique firearm in a glass case by the window, there were some assumptions you could make about how that legislator might see the world. Or, more relevant in my lobbying practice, if there was a photo on the credenza showing him in a small boat proudly holding up a trophy fish, it was a good bet he might be a problem for my commercial fishing clients.

So, my natural inclination to be diplomatic has just made me better at my job.

At least now, I was free to see if I could figure out for myself what had happened to Senator Abel Mortenson.

Chapter Three

Monday, March 1, 8:00 p.m.

A Situational Assessment

By the time the Patrol Officers left, I'd missed that hearing. Still, tomorrow I could get a detailed "blow-by-blow" from a friend who I knew would have been there. I had a lot to do before the day was out. I needed to carefully study the pile of new bills that were still being filed and to assess the progress of the several we were already tracking. Then my Associate, Janice Burdell, and her current Evergreen State College intern returned from the Hill with a detailed debrief on their work. Jan is an amazing associate, but very focused on the details. It's a great quality when you don't want something important to slip by. It can get tedious when you're pressed for time. The rest of the afternoon flew by and by the time I was finished, it was much too late to make the long commute to Seattle.

I considered texting Paula McPhee. Of late, I'd been seeing her more and more often. Paula and I had a lot in common. We'd run into each other by chance yesterday at the wedding of a mutual friend from our law school days who now lived and practiced here in Olympia. Afterwards, on our spontaneous little outing at the beach, I'd felt for the first time that we might be drawing closer.

Now, however, she'd be at home, settled in with her daughter. It was a week night; we both had work tomorrow and Marissa, an adorably precocious kid of about twelve, had school. I also wasn't entirely sure how Paula felt about me. So, instead, I just ordered dinner in from a local Chinese place and ate at my desk while I finished my work.

Then I needed to clear my head and opted for a late run. I changed into my sweats and headed downtown and into the industrial park that runs along the Olympia waterfront. The area was mostly deserted and there was very little traffic in the evening. At the marina, the rows of moored yachts were delicately suspended on glassy water that flickered with light from homes on the surrounding hills.

It had been a worrisome day; one of those days when I wondered if it had been a good choice to give up on the law to launch my lobbying practice. After my tour in the Navy, I'd put in five good years at a mid-sized Seattle law firm. I'd made a strong start at building a practice in maritime and admiralty law. I'd also been on the path to a partnership.

Back in law school, I'd fallen in love with the idea of advocating for people's rights. Seattle isn't Maycomb, Alabama, however, and I wasn't Atticus Finch. When I'd walked into my office each morning, the first things I'd see would be the unresolved client files I'd laid out on my desk the previous evening in anticipation of my next day's work. Against the far wall there'd been a big filing cabinet filled with more of those files. Each file had featured some kind of bitter confrontation. For each of them, I'd had an opponent studying my every move for some mistake, for some opportunity to torpedo me or my client. At every upcoming trial, hearing, or deposition, I could count on a face-to-face encounter with someone who, directly or indirectly, hated my guts.

There was also the inevitable emphasis on winning and on how many "billable hours" could be racked up to fuel the firm's bottom line. All of us took on too many cases to do a really sound and thoughtful job on any of them.

After five years of that, I'd hated the practice of law. Just thinking about it still made my stomach churn.

I'd put myself through college and law school by commercial fishing on my dad's boat in Alaska. I knew the commercial fishing business inside out. In the course of my law practice, one of my dad's friends had asked if I'd be interested in helping a group of local Puget Sound commercial fishermen write and then lobby a bill through the State Legislature, I'd jumped at the chance. That work had led to more, and to spending more time in the Capitol Rotunda in Olympia than at my law firm's office in Seattle. None of that would have mattered if these fishermen had been big-time clients who could pay the law firm's steep hourly rates. They weren't and I was forced to make a choice. At the time, it had been an easy one.

The last leg of my run led back up through town. I was doing fine. I enjoyed and believed in my work. My prospects looked good. My life and finances would definitely have been more stable as a partner in an established law firm. Would I have found myself a suspect in some homicide? I'd never know.

I did know that if I didn't want to lose my reputation and my practice I'd better find a way to get myself cleared. If I didn't, I also wouldn't be much use in dealing with the issues I cared about or in helping the clients I liked and respected and who badly needed my help. Mortenson's death suggested that something deeply troubling was going on beneath the surface in Olympia, something that, given Mortenson's position in the Legislature, could easily affect the fishing industry

I had to know what that was.

By ten p.m., I was in bed in the upstairs room next to my office. Despite my run, I had a restless night. Truth be known, the Senator had been a real and continuing pain. If he'd followed through on his threat to kill the gillnet/seabird gear bill, I'd have faced some very tough questions from the gillnetters, a fractious client in the best of times. I had worked with the Senator, but I sure as hell hadn't liked him, a fact that could be attested to by any number of my colleagues if they happened to be asked the right questions.

I thought I'd made a reasonably good case to Lieutenant Wilson in our interview. I was sure I'd have been recorded on the security camera when I left the Newhouse Building just after noon. That didn't let me off the hook, however. Theoretically, I could still have killed Mortenson just before leaving his office. Or returned to do so later, as stupid as that might have been.

Initially, I wondered why the State Patrol was investigating this. I'd always assumed they focused on highway traffic. It was local city police or county sheriffs that investigated murder cases. I knew the House and Senate hired Sergeants-at-Arms to guard the office buildings, but one also saw uniformed State Patrol officers on campus all the time. With a little research earlier that evening, I had learned that the WSP had jurisdiction over all crimes on the Capitol Campus. This was, however, the first murder I'd ever heard of being committed at the Capitol so it might be an unusual case for them. Although the Patrol had a sterling reputation, I hoped Wilson and his team were up to the challenge.

Police officers keep a low personal public profile; I'd been unable to learn much online about the Lieutenant. The two younger officers had been way out of their league yesterday; it wasn't clear why they'd even been present other than as witnesses or for backup. Within the WSP, a Lieutenant was a relatively senior officer. From the way he'd introduced himself, I believed Wilson was an administrator. Also, as with other police agencies, the Patrol's "detectives" typically wore civilian dress. I did, however, find an article in the *Tacoma News Tribune* from several years earlier that mentioned a TPD Detective Nathan Wilson in connection with a gang killing. That helped set my mind at ease. He'd had some solid experience in Tacoma before joining the Patrol. He'd also seemed capable, though it was hard to read him. He'd certainly been out of his depth on political and legislative issues.

I should count myself lucky that he hadn't read me my rights. If I was charged, I could probably kiss my growing government relations practice good-bye. Whatever the outcome, I knew I had not killed Senator Abel Mortenson. Now I had to convince everyone else.

I got very little sleep that night. By morning, however, I had fully resolved to see what I could learn for myself.

Chapter Four

Tuesday, March 2, 3:30 p.m.

A Prime Sponsor

Although I didn't know the first thing about investigating a murder, there wasn't anybody who knew a lot more than me about what happened behind closed doors at the Washington State Capitol. The people who worked with Mortenson, the group including the most likely suspects, were people I dealt with all the time. Maybe I could discover something about the motive for this murder by just asking a few extra questions.

I'd need to be careful. One of my friends, someone I worked with every day, could turn out to be a murderer.

Unfortunately, a manipulator like Mortenson worked in secrets. I might find it tricky identifying all the people who hated him, especially those who hated him the most. If Mortenson had dealt with others the way he'd dealt with me, there could be lots of people who might love to see him gone. Nonetheless, there were some whose dislike was obvious.

One of those people was Senator Digger Troy. I had dealt with Senator Troy a good deal. I liked the man; he had clear values and priorities. He was a Republican cattleman from Eastern Washington, who'd earned his nickname, "Digger," from his early days working the fence lines on his parent's ranch in the Okanogan Highlands and still had the shoulders to prove it. He was one of the Eastern Washington 'Rs' who could be counted on to support the commercial fishing industry. He understood business and its needs. He was a vote I'd get so long as I never wandered off message and into protecting salmon habitat. It was because of Legislators like Troy that my clients kept environmentalists at arms-length.

Most of my clients knew that it was degradation of the freshwater streams and rivers where salmon spawn and rear that was destroying the runs. You'd expect the fishermen who depended on those fish to support protecting their habitat. Individually, they often did. The minute, however, that we publicly cozied up to environmentalists, we'd be persona-non-grata with those Eastern Washington farmer-Republicans like Troy who often cast the deciding votes. This was the dirty, unspoken secret: as long as the sport-commercial fishery battles continued, none of us, on either side, could publicly and aggressively join the struggle to actually protect the fish. Similar motives rippled throughout the legislature. This was why the politics of preserving salmon habitat remained deadlocked.

I'd spoken with Troy many times about salmon harvest issues. He thought a strong economy and full employment were far more important than a few dying runs of Pacific salmon. He also hated that Pacific Northwest Indian Tribes had been awarded special rights by U.S. Federal treaty to harvest fifty-percent of those fish. One of those Tribes had a Reservation in his district. (I assumed they consistently voted for whoever opposed him.) Troy was offended that tribal members might have any special rights to catch fish or to any other "public" resource. He thought they were "coddled." He had no time for them or for most of their concerns.

Protecting salmon habitat and Tribal fishing rights were among the topics I *never* discussed with him.

Most of us who worked at the Capitol knew, Digger Troy deeply, and perhaps justifiably, resented Abel Mortenson. Mortenson was everything Troy hated. It wasn't just a matter of party. It was that to someone like Troy, whose life was guided by his firmly grounded code of ethics, Mortenson was a man without principle. Troy had served on Natural Resources Committee for several years in the minority. Most of it with Mortenson serving as Chair. He'd seen more than his fill of Mortenson. It was well known that, in caucus, Troy had organized the opposition to inviting Mortenson to join the Republicans, arguing vigorously against it. Mortenson had known that too. The vote to allow him in was a bitter pill.

Last Session, Troy was Ranking Republican on the Natural

Resources Committee. When the Republicans took power, he'd believed he'd been owed the Committee Chairmanship. By awarding that Chair to Mortenson instead, a Democrat, his Republican colleagues had effectively made Troy pay the price for their current control of the Senate. Troy had ended up chairing Agriculture, a position he felt could have gone to someone else. Natural Resources was where the fish issues went and where they sent bills that dealt with Indian fishing rights. That was where Troy had wanted his hand on the tiller. He telegraphed his resentment to any acute observer. He was high on my list of people with a motive.

I had plenty of reasons for a meeting with Troy. I was tracking several bills on which Troy's influence and vote would be important. Late morning, as I waited outside another legislator's office for a meeting, I called Troy's Legislative Assistant and was lucky to catch an appointment that same afternoon.

Senator Troy's office was on the first floor of the Newhouse Building. It was, I noted, right at the foot of the building's back stairs and directly beneath Mortenson's office up on the second floor. The Senator's Legislative Assistant was out and the door to the inner office was closed when I arrived. There was the murmur of voices coming from inside; Troy was still meeting with his earlier appointment.

I saw a paper appointment book open on the L.A.s desk; not everybody in this place had fully entered the 21st century. After carefully listening for signs of movement in Troy's office or for anyone coming down the hall, I spun the book around and quickly flipped back to the day before. Sure enough, Troy had been scheduled with appointments right up to noon on Monday. His Monday afternoon calendar had been equally full, with a Ways and Means Committee hearing right after lunch and a full Senate Session at three-thirty. A single angled line had been drawn in through both of those afternoon events—crossing them out. Something had come up at the last minute to interrupt his day. I fanned back through the pages over the past month or so and found a couple of other afternoons that had been similarly lined through.

What was that about?

At the sound of someone approaching out in the hall, I quickly flipped the page back, rotated the book to its original position, and stepped away just in time for the Senator's L.A. to come in through the outer doorway. Shortly after that, the inner office door opened; the Senator's previous appointment was departing.

The Senator's private office was a monument to the cattle industry. On a bookcase by the window, he had an incredible bronze statue of a longhorn steer, circa the mid-1800s. There was a trophy or award on his desk that featured golden spurs mounted on a walnut base. Among the items on his wall was a certificate of accomplishment from the 4-H Club awarded to Reggie Troy, who I'm reasonably sure was the Senator's son. There were several photos of Senator Troy and others on horseback and herding cattle. His wife was in several of the pictures. One of them showed Troy with his wife, their two children, and the family dogs, all posing beneath a tall "Troy Ranch" sign that stood over the entrance to their place in Okanogan County, east of the Cascade Mountains.

As I shook his hand, I renewed an offer I'd made in the past: "Are we going to get you out on one of our boats this summer, Senator? A couple of my purse seiners would love to show you how they do their job."

"Maybe so. One of these days. I'd like that. After Session. We'll see how things go."

He seemed distracted. I recalled that he was dealing with a wife who had early-onset Alzheimer's. "Maybe this fall when the season gets really rolling, we can set it up. Whenever you're able. Um, I was sorry, by the way, to hear your wife isn't well. I hope she's doing okay."

"Well, it is what it is, I guess. We take what comes," he said. "I hardly have time to get home to the ranch any more, what with being down here and keeping her company up in Seattle. She's in good hands. Maybe you know the place. Lady of the Lamp. It's just off Boren up on Pill Hill." Pill Hill is what they call the Medical District on Seattle's Capitol Hill.

I shook my head. I hadn't heard of it. If she was institutionalized over here west of the mountains she must be in worse shape than I'd realized. That brought back unhappy memories of my own, of time I'd also spent sitting helplessly next to a hospital bed beside a dying wife.

"I'm lucky to have a son who can cover the ranch," he continued.

I'd actually visited the Troy Ranch once a couple of years before. I'd been with an educational bus tour set up by the local Conservation District. The Senator hated environmentalists. He was, however, an Associate Member of his local Conservation District and a very responsible conservationist himself. He'd spoken to the bus group about how his family was cooperating with the U.S. Bureau of Land Management to systematically coordinate protection of both his private land and their adjacent public land from overgrazing. Seeing him on his own place like that, and hearing him talk about matters he cared about, it felt like we'd bonded.

The Troy Ranch was well off the main highway. A nicely-maintained gravel road followed a small stream up an impressive winding canyon until it opened out into a lovely valley in the center of which was the ranch itself. It was stunning. The white-painted home and ranch outbuildings were surrounded by a wide, fenced, pasture covering several hundred mostly level acres on both sides of the stream that ran down the center of the valley. The brown, native vegetation that covered the encircling hillsides contrasted starkly with the ranch's lush green, irrigated pasture and with a soft blue, cirrus-streaked sky. I was told you could step out their back door and hike or ride on public lands all the way to Canada.

It was easy to appreciate how someone could fall in love with such a place, with a livelihood that allowed you to live there.

The family owned the valley itself. The surrounding uplands were Federal land grazed by Troy's cattle under leases with the Bureau of Land Management or with the U.S. Forest Service. Eligibility for those leases was conditioned on ownership of adjoining private cattle lands and on the use of sound conservation management practices, which Troy applied to his own land as well as to that owned by the BLM. I found it reassuring, and, yes, a bit ironic, to see this firmly-avowed anti-environmentalist taking such pride in his own, personal environmental responsibility.

Troy's wife had been with him at the time of that visit and I'd met her as well. She was a lovely, intelligent woman. I had a good idea what he was probably going through as he watched her health erode. My wife, Susan, died in a car accident on her way home from work a few days after our first anniversary. Her death had taken nearly a week, every minute of which I would remember for the rest of my life.

"Honestly, Senator, I don't know how you do it," I said. "Your appointments schedule is as tight as anybody's in this place. You're on Rules, Ways & Means, and Natural Resources. You chair Agriculture.

You never miss a hearing or a floor session. I sure couldn't care for a sick wife and do all that. There isn't anybody here that doesn't respect you for it."

"Just doing my job, Sandy." No mention of his missing a Ways & Means meeting and the Senate Session the afternoon before. I would have to check in with Senate Committee Services and look at the Senate Journal to see if he'd been there.

We spent a few minutes discussing my bills, particularly the sport priority bill. The Senator was an easy sell. He wasn't going to support any legislation that would help a few sportsmen at the cost of catching all the harvestable salmon. He saw that as a waste. If the sports priority bill passed, even more of the fish allocated to non-Tribal fisheries would go uncaught and end up being taken by Tribal fishermen. That was something Senator Troy didn't like either. I had his vote, as I'd figured I would.

When the conversation lapsed, I asked: "So I guess you've heard about Senator Mortenson?" I pointed up above our heads to where Mortenson's office was located.

"Yep." Troy shook his head.

"I apparently had the last appointment with him before he died," I volunteered. "Had a State Patrol Lieutenant at my office for an hour-and-a-half, yesterday afternoon. I sure as hell hope they figure out who did it sooner than later."

"Uh huh."

He wasn't volunteering much. This was going to be harder than I'd expected. I definitely didn't want to alienate this man. I wasn't sure where to go with this and decided I'd better back off. "Well, uh, thanks, Senator. And all the best to your wife. We're all pulling for her."

"Sure Sandy. Thanks." Then the Senator paused, but he wasn't getting up to see me off. "You know, mentioning Senator Mortenson has me thinking. You might have a chat with that young gal they just elected to the House from up his way—Miles, Stephanie Miles. She's desperate to get some damn local food bill passed. Mortenson mentioned it. She's been all over him about it; I know for a fact he's been avoiding her. She's an ambitious one. Just sayin'..."

"Well, thanks, Senator. I'll check on that," I said, hoping I wasn't being too obvious. "I was a bit surprised when a State Patrol Lieutenant showed up at my door as the investigating officer, so I took a look at the

Code. I guess the Patrol has exclusive jurisdiction over crimes on the Capitol Campus. I bet a murder is pretty unusual for them."

"Yeah, I'd guess it's probably outside their usual line of work. They're very professional at what they do, though."

"That they are," I said, thinking I should chase down my only real acquaintance in the Patrol, Lieutenant Alexi Borichevsky, their Media and Legislative Relations Director. He might know something more about the Patrol's role in all this.

Troy interrupted my thoughts with a startling piece of information: "You know, I saw Mortenson in the hall that day. Just after noon. That help you any?"

"After noon?" I was instantly alert.

"Yeah, maybe just a few minutes after. He was headed back up the stairs to his office with a cup of coffee. After you left, he must have come down here to the coffee room. So, I guess if you were his last appointment, maybe that lets you off the hook."

"Well, I guess it can't hurt." I said. "It's all probably on the security tapes anyway. That's just about when I went out the back door heading back to my office."

"Good luck with that," he said with an ironic smile.

"With…?"

"Security camera," he said, aiming his thumb toward the hallway outside his office. "Probably wasn't working."

"Really?"

He shook his head. "Thing gets vandalized. Local kids. Come in there through the back door, spray paint it and run. Big game with them. Happens all the time."

Now I understood Lieutenant Wilson's cryptic response when I'd mentioned that camera yesterday afternoon.

Senator Troy hesitated again, but made no move to stand. Finally, he said: "I'm sure you know I wasn't any fan of Abel Mortenson."

"I do. For reasons that seem pretty easy to appreciate."

"Fact is, I just can't stand all the wheelin' and dealin' that goes on in this place." Troy held up his hand. "I know, deals are how things get done, but, it seems like we're sent here to do the right thing. Not to put people like Abel-freaking-Mortenson in positions of power."

"He could be, um, troublesome," I agreed.

He looked me in the eye. "You should know. You had to deal with him all the time in Natural Resources. You should have seen him working the folks in Rules over that bill you got to let your gillnetters keep fishin' without catching birds. That's a good bill. Simple. Necessary. Keeps people at work. Keeps the Feds out of our State's business. Doesn't cost the public a dime. But, there was Mortenson pullin' strings to hold it up. Over some kind of personal insult, was the way I heard it. Man was a plague. Those guys in Rules, all of us, we all got stuff we want to get done. Stuff we need to stop. You put someone like Abel Mortenson in place, you're just askin' for trouble. We never should have allowed that SOB to join our caucus. Voters made us the opposition party, then that's what we should do. Oppose the stuff we don't like, support the stuff we do, and leave it at that. Represent the people that voted us in, that's what I think. Let the other guys represent the people that voted them in."

"Speaking of which, you think that gillnet/bird bill is likely to move, now with him gone?"

"Oh, yeah. Nobody's going to vote against that bill now. I'm happy to nurse it along. Do what I can for you."

I thanked him and, with that, the meeting was over. With Mortenson gone and with a little nudge from Troy, our gillnet/birds bill should easily move out of Senate Rules. I was sure it would pass the Senate and I could have the Governor's signature within another few days. That was worth celebrating.

As I stood to leave Senator Troy's inner office, I happened to look over and notice a garment bag hanging on a coat rack in the corner by the couch. There was a travel case on the floor beneath it with a folded blanket laying on top. Legislators like Troy whose homes were a good distance away typically rented apartments near Olympia. With his wife sick in Seattle, I thought the Senator might be spending a few nights in a motel or even, who knew, maybe occasionally, right here on that couch in his office.

That reminded me of the lined-through afternoons in his appointments book. I realized, with his wife's health declining, Troy might have, upon occasion, just decided to drive to Seattle to visit her and had his L.A. simply cancel his afternoon events. I recalled, now that I thought about it, that Senator Troy had been absent from a Natural Resources Committee hearing a week or two back; unusual since he was so scrupulous about such things.

I felt for the man. I couldn't agree with his politics, or at least not all of them. But I did have a good sense for the seven kinds of hell he was probably going through over the health of his wife.

Troy was cut rough, but he was no fool. As I left the building, I thought about how he'd immediately understood what I was after. I couldn't quite see his feud with Mortenson as a motive for murder, but Troy had certainly been forthcoming about helping my legislation, especially the gillnet bill. I had this niggling sense that maybe I'd just been offered some kind of quid-pro-quo. As I thought about it further, however, that didn't make sense knowing how Troy viewed the late Senator Mortenson.

I had the gillnet/birds bill in hand. I had another lead. Tomorrow I'd catch up with Representative Stephanie Miles.

There was something else I was mulling over as well. Something I'd noticed earlier in Senator Troy's appointment book. While I'd been upstairs meeting with Senator Mortenson at eleven-forty-five a.m. on Monday, Senator Troy had been just downstairs meeting with his last morning appointment as well. Senator Troy had been present in the building. He knew the security camera wasn't working. He could have done the deed.

He wasn't, however, the only one.

Senator Troy's eleven-forty-five a.m. meeting on Monday had been with another prominent figure on my suspect list: Clive Curtin.

Chapter Five

Wednesday, March 3, 6:00 p.m.

Touching Base

Wednesday evening, I left early on my commute to Seattle. I'd been thinking about my dad. Dad was nearing seventy and still fishing. It was already March and, before long, he'd be cranking up the old GMC diesel in his forty-two-foot commercial salmon troller and heading north for yet another season in Southeast Alaska. After that, it would be five months before I saw him again. Five months of worry.

It was time for a visit.

It was still light as I parked at Fishermen's Terminal and headed down the long pier toward my dad's boat. The place was busy with fishermen coming and going, working in their trolling cockpits, stringing rigging, or scraping away at peeling paint. As I stood aside for one of the Terminal's heavy work carts to be wheeled past me, I heard a loud thump and then a curse from the open fish hatch on a nearby boat. Somebody's day wasn't ending well.

My dad was down on a beat-up painting float tied alongside the *Shirley J.* He was in his overalls working a quarter sheet orbital sander along his teak-oiled ironbark cap-rails. Most of the exterior painting was done and the boat looked great. Seeing it under preparation yet again for the coming thousand-mile journey to Alaska brought back a flood of memories. Throughout my early childhood, I'd yearned to join my fisherman father on that annual voyage, to spend my summers helping him catch those big, powerful salmon. Then my mom died. I was only twelve. Her long, uninsured illness had left him with no choice

28

but to sell the house, move aboard, and take me with him to Alaska the following Spring, at least three years sooner than he'd intended.

I'd lived with him aboard this boat until I'd graduated from high school. Then I'd worked my way through college and law school aboard her, at my father's side in Southeast Alaska. For years, it had been my job to sand and paint those same well-worn, freshly-coated, checker boards now drying in the last rays of the sun.

The howl of my dad's sander had masked my approach so he didn't notice me standing there taking in the scene and the smell of paint. For some strange reason, I loved the smell of paint.

Dad may be getting old, but that's never going to keep him from looking after the *Shirly J.* He counts on what he calls the "two nice weeks in February." Some years they're in late January. Some years, like now, they don't happen till early March. Some years they're not even consecutive. It doesn't matter. It's still the same "two nice weeks in February." That's when he always paints the boat.

Finally, he shut down the sander to run a hand over a patch of just-sanded rail and to cast a critical eye back along the completed section of his work. That's when he noticed me standing there on the dock.

"Sandy," he said, pulling off the paper mask that covered his lower face and greying beard. He looked back at the work for a moment, then squinted up at the dying sun. "Enough of that," he said. With a trace of regret, he laid down the sander and swung himself up off the float and onto the back deck as I stepped down off the pier. "Good to see you, son," he said, brushing some sand dust from his face and then taking my hand in his own work-hardened grip. "You should have called."

I smiled at that. "Right," I said as he smiled back. My dad never answers his phone in the middle of the day. He refuses to take it with him when he goes anywhere. When he's aboard, even if he hears it ring he just ignores it. I know never to call till the sun goes down. "I don't want to take you away from your work," I added, tossing my jacket onto the top of the fish hatch and bending down to gather up some dusty, curled up sections of worn-out sandpaper that he'd tossed aside in his progress down the cap-rail.

"No, no. Leave that," he insisted. "It's already cooling off. Getting damp. I'm done for the day."

"Boat looks great," I said. "What's this?" I knocked on one of his brand-new aluminum trolling poles. He'd done some very nice work on the rigging recently, finally bending to the inevitable and abandoning the old wooden poles. He had always sworn wood poles fished better.

"Yeah, well," he said doubtfully. "We'll see, I guess." He wouldn't have gone to all the work and expense if he hadn't been convinced, but it wasn't my dad's way to simply change his mind about a thing. Certainly not to be seen to change his mind.

We talked for a while about the boat and about the coming season. Then: "Why don't you come on in," he said, nudging my arm and guiding me toward the pilothouse door. "What brings you by? Haven't you got your hands full with those folks in Olympia? How about some coffee?"

We stepped inside the pilothouse and I took my place at the scarred Formica settee table, the same place I always took. As usual, the pilothouse was warm. The old oil stove rumbled gently in the galley; he ran it morning-to-night every day of the year, no matter what the weather.

"Sure, Dad," I said, trying hard not to betray my hesitation about the coffee. By this time, his "coffee" would have been heating and thickening on top of that stove for most of the day. No fancy Keurig coffee-makers for my dad. He liked the real thing; eggshells and all. "Actually," I continued, "I do have something of a problem."

"Problem?" He stopped in mid-reach for the two mugs that hung on hooks beneath the galley cabinet. He was instantly concerned.

"Well, a question anyway. Any chance you read about the State Senator that died? Killed in his office a couple of days ago?"

"Yeah. I did. Guy from Bellingham." He put the mugs in the counter and started filling them from the darkly stained "stainless" steel pot.

"Yeah. Senator Mortenson. He was Chair of Natural Resources— one of the committees I deal with all the time."

"He was murdered, right?"

"Right."

"You worked with him a lot, huh?"

"Uh huh."

Dad looked at me closely, reading me like a well-worn nautical chart. "What's going on, Sandy. You connected to this somehow?"

"Not really." He was watching me closely. "Except for, well… I might be something of a suspect, I guess."

The two full mugs made it to the table, but not without some spillage. He sat heavily opposite me and stared, incredulous. "A suspect?" he said.

I laid it all out. How Mortenson had died shortly after I'd left him. His involvement in fisheries issues. His key, unsettling role in the Legislature.

"So… there've got to be a whole lot of suspects, right?" My dad hates politics. But he caught on immediately. Maybe it was all about genetics, after all.

"Yeah but I'm the guy who was with him immediately before he died. We argued. I don't have an alibi." I paused a moment. "I guess I'm not all that worried for myself. It'll sort itself out. But, I know all these people, the ones that might have done it. Work with them all the time. It's hard to imagine that any of them could have done something like this."

Dad leaned back and took a sip of coffee, looking at me silently with an appraising eye. "*Anybody* could do something like this," he said, finally. He had spent two years in Vietnam back in the late sixties. Two years about which he never spoke. I had no doubt he knew exactly what he was talking about.

"I've made a list," I said. "I'm going to ask a few questions. I don't really care who did it, but I need to know what was behind it. If someone hated the man enough to kill him, there's a good chance it has to do with my work with the fishermen. Something's going on, and I don't know what it is."

I could tell he was concerned. I should never have launched this conversation. It wasn't going as I'd expected. I guess I was looking for moral support without thinking about how this was likely to affect my dad. I hadn't intended to get him worrying about me. After a moment of tension, he leaned back with his coffee, nodded as if he'd recognized some hidden truth, and smiled.

"What?" I asked.

"Still worried about the lost fish," he said.

I shook my head, questioning him.

"You never could forgive yourself when one got away," he said. "Laid awake at night worrying about it. Used to practice with the gaff when there was nothing on the line. I saw you out there. You weren't what I'd call a 'natural' at fishing. But I'll say this: You never made the same mistake twice."

"That's not what this is about, Dad. I just have an obligation to the fishermen. If there's something going on, here, I need to know what it was."

"Uh huh."

He wasn't in the least convinced, but I wasn't going to change his mind.

"One thing, though," he continued. "You start making lists and asking questions, I hope you're looking out for yourself."

"It isn't like that, Dad. I'm not going to start interrogating people. Just a little exploring, is all. See what I can figure out."

"You go bushwhacking, you need to watch for snakes, son." He gave me a thoughtful look. "You've always tended to see the best in people. But, they can surprise you. Turn on you when you least expect. You start poking around, here, you keep your eyes open, okay?"

"I will, Dad," I promised, sure, in the back of my mind, that his advice was more about some unspoken nightmare from the Mekong Delta than about my current problems in Olympia.

I refused dinner knowing he'd go to a lot of work making something "special" that he didn't personally care for. After less than an hour's visit, I was out on the dock headed back to the car.

Near the foot of the dock, I ran across one of my dad's former fishing partners, Stan Nikolic on the *Lady May*. I hadn't seen Stan for years. He was younger than my Dad, but not by much. A big guy who, even at his age, carried himself like the young buck who'd played linebacker at Ballard High School almost fifty years before. He was carrying an outboard motor slung over his shoulder like it weighed nothing. He didn't bother to set it down while we spoke.

"Well, what-a-ya-know," he said, shaking my hand vigorously with his right hand while his left balanced the motor. "Fran's boy, Sandy. Visitin' your dad, I guess."

Big Stan, standing there gripping my hand and grinning at me like we were brothers, made feel like I'd never left this place. When I was maybe fifteen, my dad had been partnered up with Stan Nikolic. We'd fished side-by-side with the *Lady May*, sharing data, calling each other when the fishing was good, and running in to town together when the trip was up. He reminded me that all this was in my blood and always would be. "Yep," I said, squinting at the faint remaining glow of the now-absent sun. "Not so long, now, I guess. You headed north again?"

"Oh yeah., Long as they let us fish, I'll be fishin'. That's why we got you, right? You keep those boys honest, we keep catchin' fish."

Stan, I recalled, was one of a breed of fishermen who are convinced the dishonest politicians in Olympia are all out to make themselves rich and, somehow in the process, to do the fishermen in. It's not so far from the truth, but not in exactly the way Stan believes. This wasn't the time, however, to explain otherwise. Not with him standing there with sixty or seventy pounds of outboard motor resting on his shoulder and a lifetime of misconceptions weighing on his brain.

"I better let you get back to your boat with that thing," I said. "Before you bust a gut."

"Ta, nothin'," He said.

"Good to see you, Stan," I said. "Take care of yourself."

"Always," he said. "You too. You tell those assholes down there in Olympia to look out. Last thing they want is for us boys to come down there our own selves and straighten them out."

I sincerely hoped that never happened. Big Stan Nikolic was as good a reason as any I could think of why these guys needed me running interference for them down in Olympia.

That's why I needed to understand why Abel Mortenson had been murdered.

Chapter Six

Wednesday, March 3, 9:00 a.m.

A Failed Motion

Okay, I probably should have left well enough alone.

My condominium in Seattle was only a few blocks from the financial district. The morning after my visit with my dad was clear and warm. I had nothing scheduled in Olympia. I headed downtown on foot for what I hoped might be an informative impromptu conversation with Clive Curtin.

I gave some careful thought to my approach while I walked. I didn't want to confront him directly. I needed an excuse. The current, widely publicized stalemate in negotiations between the Department of Fish and Wildlife and the Northwest Tribal Fisheries Consortium might fit that bill. At the moment, it looked like all salmon fishing, sport, commercial, and Tribal, might be delayed, this year, because of that State-Tribal disagreement. Clive and I could look for ways to work together, share information, try to bring the parties together. Once I was in Clive's door, I'd find some segue to Mortenson and what Clive knew about his death.

I'd heard Curtin was a successful insurance broker. His firm's website had certainly been professional. Until I stepped out of the elevator some two-thirds of the way to the top of the Columbia Center, however, I'd had no idea. On the wall, just outside the elevator door, there was a walnut placard with huge raised bronze letters that read: "Curtin and Associates, Insurance Brokers." Beneath that, in slightly smaller script: "Life, Health, Property, Casualty." The firm's reception desk was visible through heavy, double glass doors that opened directly off of the elevator lobby; it looked like they occupied an entire floor of what had to be among the costliest office spaces in town. I knew from my own experience that some of the most successful law firms in Seattle couldn't afford the rents in this building.

The Columbia Center is modern and austere in greys and glass. As I stepped into the Curtin and Associates reception area, I saw all that gave way to exotic polished hardwoods, tasteful burgundy oriental carpets, and plush old-world furniture. Clearly Clive Curtin had done well for himself.

There was another big surprise. I wasn't the only person here for a visit this morning. Standing by and seated on a couch in the waiting area were the three musketeers from Monday's visit at my office in Olympia. The trio was hard to miss in all their State Patrol uniformed glory.

They weren't missing anything either, including me. So much for my plan to check out Clive's office and catch him in a free moment with a few questions.

Lieutenant Wilson was the one of the three who had remained standing. He narrowed his eyes. "Dalton," he said. He didn't seem especially pleased to see me there.

"Lieutenant." I said, extending my hand with a smile. "I guess we must be here to see the same person?"

Seeing them here in Clive Curtin's imposing office gave me the chills. They were about to be escorted in to hear Curtin's point of view. I momentarily wondered how these posh surroundings might impress someone who managed on what had to be a modest State salary. Would it make Curtin more credible, or less?

"What's your business, here, Mr. Dalton," Wilson finally asked.

"Salmon," I said. "Clive and I have a lot to talk about." I was reasonably sure the three Patrol Officers had an appointment. I, on the other hand, did not.

"I very much hope you're not here interfering in an official police investigation."

I wondered why he'd think that, and then recalled my conversation the day before with Senator Troy. His bluntness caught me off guard. "Interference is the very last thing I have in mind, Lieutenant," I said.

"I hope so. You need to stay clear of this matter, Dalton." His tone and body language caused his two junior officers to rise from their seats on the couch and stand beside their superior. "We'll get to the bottom if this. Whatever we discover, I hope I don't find out that you've been meddling."

That was certainly clear. Still, as far as he knew, I could be here to discuss some salmon harvest bill. "You know, Lieutenant," I said. "A lot of the people you're going to be talking to about your case are likely to be the same people I deal with every day in my work. I hope you appreciate that. But, whatever happens, I definitely plan to stay out of your way."

"I hope so."

"Absolutely," I said. "I need you to succeed at this. As you're probably already aware, Senator Mortenson had a lot going on. I'm sure you're already coming up with a whole long line of people who had way more reason to dislike the Senator than I ever would." Doing my best to seem genuinely helpful, I continued, making it an afterthought: "You know, if you should decide you could use my assistance in any way, I hope you'll bear in mind that I'm more than willing. Either way, please don't worry, I won't be interfering with your work."

Clive had just stepped into the waiting room, presumably to escort his guests in to his office. Now wasn't going to be a good time for us to meet. I'd also lost the element of surprise.

I turned and extended my hand. "Hey, Clive," I said, as he hesitantly took my hand. "Looks like you're busy now. I'd like to talk as soon as you get some time."

Then, ignoring Clive's confused look, I turned back to Lieutenant Wilson and his troopers, gave them a little nod and a friendly smile, and exited back out through the big glass doors, leaving them all behind.

Chapter Seven

Wednesday, March 3, 9:30 a.m.

Unsolicited Support

Lieutenant Nathan Wilson was a man to be taken seriously. As I headed back to my Seattle condo to get my car, I reflected on his warning not to get involved. I wasn't sure I even knew what might constitute "interfering with a police investigation" or what the penalties might be. As I considered what I'd discussed in yesterday's conversation with Senator Troy, I hoped that wouldn't be seen as already crossing some line. My understanding had always been that "obstruction of justice" or "interfering in a police investigation" involved some kind of affirmative wrongdoing like intimidating a witness, misleading the police, or destroying evidence. I had no plans to do any of that.

It was frustrating. I was a lobbyist. How was I supposed to do my job if I couldn't talk to people? I had to know what was going on behind the scenes. The important stuff, the personal things people didn't discuss in public. Those were often the things that drove their votes. Knowing those things was how I figured out what people cared about, what would work and what wouldn't, where to push, which topics to avoid, how to make friends and avoid enemies. It would take some careful footwork to stay out of trouble and still find this murderer.

Somebody had murdered a Washington State Senator, for Christ's sake! Right in the man's office at the State Capitol. It might easily have been someone I knew and worked with. I didn't have the first clue to who. Or, more importantly, why. It was my business to know what the hell was going on.

On the sidewalk by the Westlake Center, I caught a text from Dean Miles suggesting that I check my email. Dean was a manager at the MFS store in Bellingham. MFS, or Maritime Fisheries Supply, was one of the major commercial fisheries supply houses. He was also on the campaign committee we'd formed to fight a statewide ballot initiative for which the sports fishing community was currently gathering signatures on street corners and in malls and park-n-rides all across Washington. Essentially, the initiative was another version of the sports-priority legislation the anglers had been unable to pass through the legislature for several years. If the initiative passed, it was going to cause huge problems for us. My role as the industry's lobbyist y extended to helping my clients avoid that.

When I brought up Dean's email on my phone, it just said: "Take a look at this!" The attachment was a .pdf copy of another email, a letter on the letterhead of the WSSC, the Washington Sports Salmon Coalition, the principal sponsor of the ballot measure, we were opposing. It was signed by Clive Curtin himself. As I walked, I scanned it with increasing interest.

My car was in the garage under my condo building. I was so engrossed in that letter when I got there that I got in and, rather than starting up and heading for Olympia, I just sat back and reread the email more carefully.

Damn! This letter could be a game changer.

The original addressees' names and email addresses had been deleted. And it wasn't at all clear from the most recent sender's complicated email address who the it was that had forwarded the message and to whom that forward had been sent. But the original author was clearly shown in the letterhead and in the signature. It was dated in Mid-November of last year.

It read:

- CONFIDENTIAL -

As a recognized leader in Washington's sports fishing community, your input and support is needed in a cause which is close to the heart of every angler. As you know, sportsmen have fought for years to secure fair access to our treasured salmon resource. We have offered reasonable solutions to

the harvest managers at the Department of Fish
and Wildlife. We have fought for equitable harvest
allocation at the Pacific Fisheries Management
Council. And we have repeatedly sought legislation
requiring fair harvests for recreational fisheries.
All of these efforts have failed in the face of an
intransigent and politically powerful commercial
fishing industry lobby.

It is time to turn the tables. We need to present
this issue directly to the Washington voting public
by statewide ballot initiative.

The attached is the draft ballot measure we're
proposing to file in January for placement on the
general election ballot next fall. It is entitled the
"Washington Salmon Protection Act" and would
expressly prohibit the use of any fishing gear
employed in the harvest of salmon that is not
capable of selectively taking salmon of a targeted
type or species without mortality to non-target
salmon in excess of twenty-five percent of those
non-targeted fish captured and released.

This was the measure they'd ended up filing with the Secretary
of State on the 10th of January and for which they were now out
gathering signatures. The twenty-five percent figure was a catch-and-
release mortality level that could be achieved in sports fisheries, but
was unattainable for most commercial net gear.

With its spiffy title: "The Washington Salmon Protection Act,"
and its clever language, the measure sounded great. Anyone living
in the Pacific Northwest knew that the habitat in many of the rivers
and streams where salmon spawn had been badly damaged. Some
runs of the fish were in trouble—in some cases even listed under the
Endangered Species Act. Other runs were quite healthy, however,
and perfectly capable of sustaining strong fisheries. Those included,
of course, the runs that were artificially raised in fish hatcheries
specifically for the purpose of being caught. The problem was that out
at sea and in salt water, where most of the fishing occurred, the fish
from all these runs tended to mix together.

Sportsmen generally kept keep the hatchery fish they caught (and which could be identified by a small clipped fin) while releasing—hopefully unharmed—wild fish that might come from runs that could not sustain much harvest. On its face, this initiative looked to be designed to help them do that, but it would actually also end all the commercial fisheries that might catch any of the fish, healthy runs and weak.

It all sounded great in theory, but it ignored the simple, critical fact that the very efficiency of commercial net gear made it far more selective than sport when constrained to limited times and places where the only fish present to be caught were from strong, healthy runs.

To be of any value to the participants, a sports fishery had to be spread out broadly across large geographic areas and conducted during long, open periods of time. So, their actual impact on non-targeted, weak salmon runs was still much higher than for commercial gear. This ballot initiative went way beyond just helping sportsmen catch hatchery fish. It was designed to eliminate commercial fishing entirely, leaving the extra fish, hatchery and non-hatchery, for sportsmen to catch.

It was, in other words, a clever ruse.

Given that, it was with increasing amazement that I read on as Clive Curtin's letter specifically explained the strategic political thinking behind their measure:

> Our polling shows the public will not vote for a straight reallocation of salmon harvests from commercial to sports fisheries. Instead, we need a measure that will decisively shift salmon harvest to anglers while presenting the matter in a way the public can support.
>
> There is deep public concern about declines in our salmon resource. The attached initiative is designed to appeal to that concern while producing a reallocation of the catch to recreational fishermen. The initiative accomplishes this indirectly by eliminating non-tribal commercial salmon net gear which cannot meet a twenty-five percent catch-

and-release mortality standard while preserving sport hook and line gear, which can.

We will argue for our initiative as a tool to protect weak runs of salmon from overharvest. Since salmon harvests are managed on pre-season forecasts and catch is allowed on the predicted surplus above those needed to regenerate the runs, actual total catch numbers should remain about the same. But eliminating the commercial fisheries will leave a great many fish that can then be taken in recreational fisheries.

The letter went on to encourage everyone to support the measure and was signed by Clive Curtin, President, Washington Sports Salmon Coalition

My brain was swirling with questions as I made my hour-long drive down I-5 to Olympia. Now that I'd seen this letter, I was glad my meeting this morning with Clive had misfired. When I next talked with Clive, I wanted to have fully sorted out its impact. My first question was: How stupid could Curtin be to have written such a thing? I supposed that, back in November, before they'd even filed their measure, he'd been focused mostly on getting support from his sports fishing colleagues and wasn't yet thinking about the public campaign they'd need next fall to get the thing passed. Whatever the explanation, this letter was dynamite. It was going to make a lot of people angry—most of all, the environmentalists. This letter was likely to move the environmental community squarely to our side of the coming battle—a very big deal.

Why was I getting this from Dean Miles; where'd he get it? Then I knew the answer. Of course! Dean was the husband of State Representative Stephanie Miles who was already on my list to talk to about the Senator's murder. Stephanie was a "D" recently elected from the 42nd District, up in Whatcom County—the House Member Senator Troy had mentioned to me the day before. Dean must have gotten it from her.

But where did she get it?

Clearly this had originally come from someone in Olympia. But who?

Chapter Eight

Thursday, March 4, 7:30 a.m.

Strategic Alliances

Wednesday morning was clear with a chilly, northerly breeze as I waited beneath the north portico of the Capitol Building for Stephanie Miles. I used the time to track some of the new bill filings on my phone and to text my associate, Janice, with some instructions for the coming day. I had Janice tracking down and cementing in floor votes on the seabird bill.

From the top of the big stairs, I could see out across the flag plaza where, after a couple of days at half-staff in honor of the fallen Senator, the flags of the United States and of the State of Washington were back at the top of their poles. Beyond the flags and the Members parking lot, was the somewhat ironically named "Temple of Justice," the building that housed the Washington State Supreme Court.

As a young law student, arguing cases in that building had seemed the pinnacle of my ambitions. During my first few years in law practice I'd spent long hours in the library researching adopted laws for clues to their meaning or intent, clues that might support my firm's argument for a client's position in that and other courtrooms. Today, that kind of research seemed almost silly. Given what I now knew about the happenstance manner in which those laws actually got passed, who could guess what a legislative body intended, or even any individual legislator? As I saw it, my current lobbying would be much more likely to influence the course of human events than any subsequent "legislative intent" research that might be done by some devoted lawyer, no matter how enterprising and creative their work might be.

As I waited and re-checked the Legislative web-page on my phone, I saw what I had anticipated. With Senator Mortenson gone, the previous Senate calendar and all Senate hearings had been temporarily cancelled. The Senate Democrats were scheduled for caucus this morning, then the Senate would be in Session again in the early afternoon.

Big changes were in the wind.

I'd spent a good part of yesterday afternoon thinking about the status of the State Patrol's investigation into Senator Mortenson's death. If I was to believe the evening news, there'd been no real progress. The minute I'd seen that message from Dean Miles, yesterday, I knew I needed to talk to his wife about it. While I was at it, though, I was sure as hell going to ask her about the bill Troy had mentioned, and see how she was reacting to Mortenson's death.

I knew Representative Stephanie Miles' parking spot and I knew what time she usually showed up for work. So, when I saw her space was empty, I simply waited, hoping to catch her early. I caught up with her in the lot below just as she was getting out of her car. She readily agreed to chat while I walked her up to her office in the O'Brien Building.

Stephanie was in her first term in the Legislature and seemed to be taking to it well. She was a tall, attractive blonde; good looks are always useful for a politician. She appeared to enjoy her work and the people around her. It all put you at ease. At the same time, she also came across as thoroughly focused and professional so one quickly forgot her appearance and how unusually young she was to be an elected state legislator. She stuck to the issue, so you did too.

It's very hard to miss the fact that Stephanie Miles is going places.

"Have you seen the letter I gave Dean?" she said, obviously knowing exactly why I was there. As we had hoped, Stephanie was turning out to be a reliable ally of the commercial fishing fleet. My commercial fishermen were among her strong supporters. I knew Dean fairly well, since he'd been active in fish politics on behalf of MFS for several years. I'd helped to arrange one of the fundraiser events in her election campaign.

"I did. He scanned it and sent it to the whole committee," I said. "Thank you, Steph. That letter is going to be a big help"

"It's a bit startling to see the sports guys' underhanded motives all spelled out in their own words."

"It sure is. We're already getting it out to the environmental community. They're going to be very unhappy to see these people using a fake environmental argument as an excuse to advance their own self-interest."

"Good," she said.

"I do, however, have a question," I said.

Stephanie laughed. "I think I know what that is. You'd like to know where I got it, right?"

"Well, yeah. If it's something you can tell me."

"At this point I'm sure it's perfectly okay. It came from Senator Mortenson."

"Mortenson?" Now that was a surprise.

"Judith Bosch, his LA, gave it to me. We had lunch last Friday."

"Judith?" I questioned. She had been Mortenson's loyal Legislative Assistant for many years.

"Yeah. We're friends. She was my Social Studies teacher in high school. We've stayed in touch."

"Do you know how Mortenson ended up with it?"

"No, but it was a forward. Probably from someone Clive Curtin thought was an ally. He's is going to be very displeased with whoever did that."

I had to laugh. "I'd say so."

"But, you know, it makes one wonder," Stephanie continued. "Mortenson had it for quite a while before Judith gave it to me. She says he received it back in November. He sees you all the time. Why didn't he just hand it over to you himself? Why'd he wait? What was he planning to do with it?"

She was right. It did make one wonder. "He and I were on the outs, the past week or so," I said. "But before that, we were getting along fine." I gave that some thought. "Wouldn't expect Abel Mortenson to just sit on something like that. He'd have had something up his sleeve, been working some kind of angle, maybe saving it as ammunition."

"Uh huh."

"You don't think he could have been holding it over Clive Curtin's head, maybe as leverage for something?"

Now Stephanie laughed. "Sounds like Abel to me."

"Me too," I laughed as well. "I gather you and Senator Mortenson were pretty close."

"Yeah, we were. He was a huge help to me. He was the first person I talked to when I decided to run. He endorsed me, let me use his lists, introduced me to some of his best donors, and hosted a great fund-raiser. All but got me elected."

"I know. He was important to us as well."

We looked at one another for a moment, perhaps thinking the same thing: that, as useful and important as Mortenson had been to each of us, probably neither one of us was truly sorry to see him go.

"Looks like some big changes over in the Senate." Stephanie motioned toward the Cherberg Senate Office Building, just ahead as we came up the sidewalk along the east side of the Capitol.

"I'm surprised they didn't caucus yesterday. Or even Tuesday, for that matter. Maybe they needed to make sure none of the conservative 'Ds' were looking to slip into Mortenson's place."

"Quite a shake-up." She paused thoughtfully. "I couldn't believe it when Abel decided to switch sides in January. I knew he was conservative, but to switch caucuses like that… After all those years as a Democrat."

I knew exactly how she felt. "Once you're elected, I guess you can call yourself anything you want and caucus with whomever you want."

"Yeah, I guess."

"Look, here's the thing," I said. Wilson or no, I needed some answers. "I think you and I may have something in common. As it happens, I had the last meeting with Abel, just before lunch the day he was killed. And we had an argument. Now the State Patrol investigators probably have me down as a suspect."

We had arrived at the O'Brien Building elevators and there were several people waiting in the hall. "Why don't you come on up?" she offered. We were both silent in the crowded elevator as we rode up to the top floor and then walked through the busy upstairs hallway.

We were in her office with the door closed before she continued: "You were saying, we have something in common?"

"I think you may get a call from them as well. From the State Patrol."

"The State Patrol?"

"Well, like me, I guess, you may have had a reason to be a bit peeved with Abel Mortenson of late. I understand he was holding up your local food thing, the Public Harvest bill."

"Wow, no secrets in this place!"

After speaking with Digger Troy the day before, I'd read her bill. I was impressed. The idea behind it was simple but neat: The bill would authorize and encourage State agencies and local governments to allow the low-cost agricultural lease of small underused and undeveloped publicly-owned lands—especially in near-urban areas. There was a surprising amount of open land that ended up in public ownership for a variety of reasons. Many of these properties could easily be rented out to local farmers and cultivated for food crops that would be grown for sale at local farmers' markets or in other in-state direct-market venues. It all seemed like a win-win for taxpayers and for the public.

Stephanie grinned. "There's not much that gets past you, eh Sandy?"

"It looks like a good bill. What's the problem?"

"It *is* a good bill. I've already got it through the House so I know it has legs. I've got a lot of local food advocates in my district. They love it. They're a rapidly growing constituency."

"How about the 'Rs?' " I asked. "Seems like you might also draw some votes from the fiscal conservatives who hate publicly owned land."

"I have. We had a very nice bipartisan majority in the House."

"This your first one—your first prime sponsorship?"

"First of many, I hope," Stephanie said. "I need to build a reputation. I don't plan to stay a State Representative forever. This bill is going to be a great start."

"So, what went wrong?"

She grimaced. "Senate Leadership assigned it to Ag Committee instead of Local Government. Senator Troy wouldn't give it a hearing."

"Why would he care? It's more land for farmers to farm. Less land maintenance cost drawing down the public purse. Some lease income to lighten the load on taxpayers. Seems like something he'd like."

"He thinks it's 'silly.' At least that's what Judith told me. She says Troy thinks the whole thing with local food is a passing fad. Figures 'foodies' are a bunch of coddled city people who should buy their 'fresh fruits and nuts' in the supermarket like everybody else. He thinks the bill would cost too much to administer."

"I see." It did make some sense. Troy's constituents were, after all, mostly big ag. Farmers who sold to big wholesalers. There couldn't be a lot of farmers' markets in Okanogan County.

"He's wrong about the admin cost. Our fiscal note was very modest."

"With Abel Mortenson being your mentor, I bet you asked him to work his magic on Senator Troy—maybe change Troy's mind."

"I never even got the chance. The minute Troy turned it down for a hearing, Abel was suddenly too busy to see me. No appointments available. He seldom shows up at the Members Cafeteria for lunch; works in his office and refuses to be interrupted. I tried to catch him on the Senate Floor during recess but he was all busy talking with other Members. All I got was a stupid grin and a helpless shrug. I need that hearing. The next action cutoff is in a few days; that bill needs to get out of committee. Abel had to know that, but something was up. He was avoiding me on purpose."

"So, what was that about? I wouldn't think Troy really cares about it all *that* much. They're not the best of friends, but Mortenson must have had something to offer that might have changed Troy's mind."

"I guess Abel just didn't want to look foolish in front of all his new Republican buddies."

"Judith told you this?"

"Yeah. She's been disappointed in him since he made the big caucus switch. It's why she gave me that letter to pass along. She was actually thinking about quitting. She's also got a lot on her mind. Her dad's a dairy farmer. He's getting along in years but he refuses to sell out. She worries about him, would like to be at home to help him but she needs the job. It's tough."

"Her dad's in Bellingham, right? Olympia's a long way from Bellingham."

"Closer to Lynden. Even further. Anyway, I asked her about Abel. She says Abel was just embarrassed about supporting the bill. All those Republicans have given him a lot of clout, like that nice end office in the Newhouse Building even though they've made the building a kind of Republican enclave. They let him keep his precious Chairmanship on Natural Resources; you know, before he switched, the Democratic Leadership was already frustrated with him. They were on the verge of giving that Chairmanship to Jimmy Fang. It's probably the main reason he went over to the dark side." Stephanie made a face and shook her head. "I guess Abel was glad to help me as long as I let him look down the front of my blouse, and as long as I wasn't asking for much. As soon as there was a price to pay, he turned out to be worthless. When push came to shove, he just wanted to look cool to all his new friends."

The whole thing seemed about as I might have expected. It did sound like Representative Miles might have had a motive to have killed the man—with the 'Ds' taking power and Mortenson gone, there'd now be a new Ag Committee Chair. But, I wasn't entirely convinced her foundering local food bill was such a big deal. It wasn't like its failure would ruin her life or her future in politics.

"Well," I said. "I just thought you might like to know that the word's out there about your bill. Mortenson talked about it. From everything I've seen, the State Patrol is pretty desperate to find a culprit."

"I can imagine. Patrol's got its image to live up to. This is big news. I assume you saw yesterday's *Seattle Times*."

I had. There'd been detailed front page coverage as well as an editorial comment focused on the troubling fact that, in this day of terrorists and gun violence, not even the office of a Washington State Senator was safe. They made a big deal about the lack of progress in the investigation and asking how something like this could happen in the middle of a busy workday, while the killer walks away without anyone seeing a thing.

"They do need to find someone to pin this on," I said, "and quickly."

"You think I could be a target?"

"Given how Mortenson worked, I think there could be a lot of targets. But, I think we might both be, let's say, 'under consideration.' Half my clients would walk out the door the minute they thought I was suspected in something like this. Not many legislators will want to invite a suspected knife murderer into their office for a private chat."

She looked at me and wiggled her eyebrows in faux alarm. "Should I be worried?"

"Nope." I smiled. "Should be okay as long as you vote for all my bills."

Then she shook her head. "Seems hard to believe someone could think I'd kill the man. After all the help, he's been to me." Stephanie gave that some further thought. "Be nice to nip this in the bud, though. 'Knife murderer' doesn't sound like a great sound-bite for a politician either."

"That's what I thought."

"You have an alibi?"

"Not really."

"Hmm. Unfortunately, I don't think I do either. Was off-campus at the time, over at the Capitol Mall doing some shopping. Nobody's going to remember me." She gave this some further thought. "I don't even think I used my credit card. Paid cash for some socks for Dean. Bought a hot dog at one of those mobile stands. Mostly just wanted to get away from the Capitol for an hour or so."

"I'm no better off," I said. "After my appointment, I walked back to the office. Nobody there to back me up. Digger Troy saw Mortenson alive after I left. But, I could have returned later. So, it's not all that solid." I consciously didn't mention that the Newhouse Building's back-door security camera had been down. I did wonder if she knew about it.

As I stood to leave, Stephanie grinned: "I never got a chance to ask you how it went with Dean's friend, Carol." For some reason, Stephanie had taken it into her head that I needed a wife or at least a girlfriend. A few months earlier, before I'd started getting serious about Paula, Stephanie and Dean had lined me up with one of Dean's fellow employees at MFS in Bellingham. It had been a very nice date. But the distance between there and Olympia was a bit far for any serious relationship.

"A nice young woman," I said. "We enjoyed ourselves immensely."

"Oh," said Stephanie, looking disappointed. "I see. Well, don't worry about it. I won't be giving up on you any time soon."

"Believe me, I'm not worried," I replied with a smile. "I didn't expect that you would."

As I made my way back outside, I thought about our conversation. It was certainly friendly enough. She'd been more than cooperative, conspiratorial almost, in her answers. But, she really hadn't given me anything solid concerning her own situation, other than that she didn't have an alibi. Her revelations about Clive Curtain, seemed almost designed to make me look elsewhere.

I didn't really need much encouragement to suspect Clive. But, I wasn't entirely convinced about the complete innocence of Representative Stephanie Miles either.

Chapter Nine

Thursday, March 4, 1:30 p.m.

Parliamentary Inquiry

One big surprise from my conversation with Stephanie Miles was that the Clive Curtin letter had come from Judith Bosch. Judith had obviously also revealed to Stephanie a good deal of insider detail on Mortenson's thinking about Stephanie's bill. Judith had stuck by Mortenson for years. Never, not once, had I sensed anything from her other than complete devotion to her boss. Maybe they were good friends, as Stephanie had said. Still, for Judith to do something behind Mortenson's back like that seemed very unusual.

There was too much happening that I didn't understand. It all swirled around Abel bloody Mortenson. I still wanted to have that chat with Clive Curtin. First, however, I needed to talk to Judith Bosch. As it concerned the sportsmen's initiative, I felt I would have a right to ask questions about it. Lieutenant Nathan Wilson wasn't the only person with a job to do.

Judith Bosch worked for Mortenson year-round. During session, she was his Legislative Assistant. Off session, she returned to Bellingham and staffed his District Office. For several months every four years, when not officially employed in one or the other of those jobs, she helped to staff his periodic re-election campaigns. What with scheduling my frequent appointments with her boss, greeting me in the Senator's outer office, passing along my messages, acting as intermediary for me and my clients off session at Mortenson's local district office, and even enlisting my help on fundraisers and for Mortenson's many appearances at commercial fishing industry events,

Judith Bosch had probably had more contact with me over the years than had the Senator himself.

Judith had started out as a Social Studies teacher at Sehome High School near Bellingham. She'd taught classes in U.S. Government, Contemporary World Problems, and Economics and, for many years, she'd been active in the 42nd District Democrats as well as in the local council of the Teachers Union. When she'd received the offer to come work for the Senator, she'd apparently been itching for years to actually practice some of what she'd been teaching. She'd wanted to become a "part of the action." I'm not sure that's what she ended up with, but she'd never gone back to the classroom and she was both good at and seemed satisfied in her job.

With Senator Mortenson gone, Judith would probably be unemployed. Technically, she worked for the State so I wasn't clear exactly what would happen with her job. I asked a friend in Senate Committee Services and was told that Judith might actually be staying on temporarily and moving over, for the balance of the Session, to a position in Natural Resources Committee staff. After taking Tuesday and Wednesday off, Judith had come back in today to try to "clean up" some of Senator Mortenson's office work. His replacement was still to be nominated by the local Democratic Party with final selection by the Whatcom County Council. She had wanted to start getting things organized in preparation for the new Senator.

The door to Mortenson's office in the Newhouse Building was closed and "sealed" with a "crime scene" notice taped to the thick oak door. When I knocked tentatively, I heard movement inside and, after a moment, Judith herself opened the door.

"Any chance we could talk for a moment?" I asked.

"Sure, Sandy. Come on in." Seeing my glance at the "crime scene" notice, she said: "Oh, don't worry about that." She reached up and pulled the paper off the door. "The State Patrol technical people are all done here. They said to just go ahead and ignore it."

It seemed strange to step into this office knowing what had occurred here only three days earlier. The door to Mortenson's inner office was open. His desk looked exactly as it had when I'd been here on Monday and on the many other previous occasions over the years. Judith went around and sat behind her desk in exactly the place I'd seen her sit through several legislative sessions as well. As I sat in one of the guest chairs, it felt as if the Senator himself might materialize at any moment.

Then a faint whiff of very real disinfectant drifted lightly out through the inner office door and reminded me that he was definitely gone for good.

She looked puzzled by my presence. "I'm, ah, hoping you can help," I said. "As you know, Abel and I had a bit of an argument before he died on Monday…"

Her face cleared. "Oh Sandy," she said, and smiled. "Of course, I told them about your argument, but I wouldn't think for a moment you'd have killed the man. You and he have worked together for years. He always, well, had a lot going on. In the end, he mostly came through for you, as you know. He was a difficult man, no doubt about that. He was, I guess, *our* difficult man, if you know what I mean."

That was exactly how I would have put it. "It must have been horrible, finding him like that," I said.

It was a probably a clumsy thing for me to have said because she noticeably paled at the recollection. "I… I've never seen anything like that," she said. "It didn't look real. Just for a moment I thought it was some kind of faked thing, a joke or something. Like some show on TV. God, Sandy. He was stabbed." Another pause. "His own knife."

The papers had mentioned stabbing. But, I didn't know it had been with Mortenson's own knife. I thought about that. "You mean that big Lummi knife he kept on his desk." The heirloom ceremonial knife had been a prominent feature on Mortenson's desk. It had been a gift from the Lummi Tribe made some years before, in better times.

"Uh huh."

"I'm so sorry," I said, not knowing what else to say to that. It was interesting, though, because the use of that knife suggested the killing might have been spontaneous. "I guess you'd gone to lunch by the time the Senator and I were done talking," I continued.

"I was at Smiley's with some friends." Smiley's was a salad and sandwich shop along Capitol Way toward downtown Olympia. "As I told the Lieutenant, I left right at noon. You guys were still in there when I left."

"How about when you came back. He was in the office, right?"

"Yeah. Door was closed. Couldn't hear any voices so I figured he was in there working. I knocked and he didn't answer. I opened it up and…" She took a deep breath.

"You're the one that called the Patrol?"

"No. I don't know who that was. Maybe the Sergeant at Arms from downstairs. He was here right after."

"You must have been here when they arrived."

"Uh huh. They made me wait out in the hall. Wouldn't let me go back in, even to get my purse and jacket. I needed to lay down. I finally went downstairs to Janice Liverpool's office. She has a couch in her waiting room. Laid down for a while, until I felt better. Went home early."

"So, you probably don't know much about what they found, at the scene I mean?"

"No, Sandy. As I said, I was out in the hall. Then I went downstairs."

"I see."

"I did hear the coroner say that he couldn't be sure if Abel had actually died immediately. Something to do with a spinal injury. He said he needed to do the autopsy, but that Abel might have been unconscious and maybe just sat there bleeding in his chair. I can't get over the thought that he could have been in there bleeding and needing help or something while I was off enjoying lunch."

"Did they say anything about when they thought he died?"

"You mean like, time of death, right?"

I nodded.

"No. I didn't hear anything about that."

I was thinking that if they had pinned a time of death for later in the lunch hour, that might help my case. If they didn't know how quickly he'd died, time of death wouldn't necessarily pin down when the crime had been committed.

Then I asked: "Judith, I spoke earlier with Stephanie Miles. She told me it was you that gave her that letter from Clive Curtin, the one about their ballot initiative. I'd guess with the Senator gone, maybe you don't mind that she did that. I hope not. I'm sure that's what she was thinking. I want you to know we appreciate having it. We owe you for that. If you don't want it known, I will be happy to keep it confidential."

Judith looked uncomfortable for a moment. But then said: "No, really, I can't see how it matters at this point. I was feeling a bit disloyal to do it, is all. I guess it doesn't make any difference now."

"Would you mind telling me why you did?"

"Sandy, you know I owed a lot to Abel Mortenson. But that letter— that's the kind of thing that should be made public."

"Still, the two of you go way back, right?"

She smiled. "You could say that. I taught his son in the tenth grade." She shook her head. "A long time ago."

"He has a son? I didn't know that."

"It was by a first marriage. Didn't last long. He and his ex-wife got shared custody. She wasn't much of a mother. Even though Abel remarried, he and the son have maintained a relationship over the years. That's how I first met Abel. He came to a parent-teacher conference and we got talking politics. Later, when I was with the Washington Teachers Union, I met him again at a fundraiser. Then, a few months later, he called to offer me this job. I think Dougie now lives in Seattle, Ballard area. Repairs boats or something." She smiled again at the recollection. "As a boy, he wasn't much of a student, but he sure loved boats."

"I'd guess you probably kept a few secrets for the Senator over the years. I bet there were lots of times there would have been public impact from disclosing them. Why this? What made you want to reveal this one in particular?"

Now Judith was looking uncomfortable again. She hesitated, but then seemed to come to a conclusion. "Okay, I'll tell you why. He was using it for leverage. Personal interest again. Maybe you haven't heard, but he was going to face a serious primary challenge in the next election. You know our Whatcom County Assessor, Phil Sheridan? Won reelection last time around with something like sixty-five percent of the vote, a thirty-point spread. He's been considering a run for the Senate. Now, with Abel gone, he'll run for sure. He'll almost certainly get the interim appointment to Abel's seat. He would have given Abel a hell of a time in the primary, and in the general if Abel had run as an independent which, if he'd lost the primary, I'm sure he would have done."

"Okay," I hadn't heard about that, but it made sense. Democratic loyalists hated Abel Mortenson, and Sheridan was very well-liked.

"Anyway, he'd held onto that letter for over three months without letting anybody know. I saw it back when it came in on his email; I see everything he gets. I kept wondering when he was going to let you guys know. He'd have to, sooner or later. Then, about a week ago, he had Clive Curtin in here. That door isn't as thick as you might think. But, on this occasion, they didn't even shut it completely. I heard the whole conversation. The Senator wanted Curtin's endorsement in the next election. Wanted the sportsmen's vote. You know, Sandy, there are a lot of anglers in the 42nd District. Abel was pretty loyal to your commercial guys, but it was never an open-and-shut case. He could just as easily have gone the other way. Here he was, possibly doing just that. Or, if not, he was at least trying to soften up their opposition."

With that, a lot of pieces fell into place. I'd been a bit surprised that Mortenson had been so brazen in blocking the gillnet/bird bill, and that he'd turned so negative over that mild commentary I'd published in the newsletter. Maybe he had been considering a change of horses. What had stopped him? If this was true, why had he folded when I'd pressured him over the newsletter stuff in our final meeting on Monday? Perhaps he'd still been making up his mind.

"You said he was using Curtin's letter as leverage?"

"Yeah, or maybe 'blackmail' might be the better term. I gathered he'd previously asked Curtin to publish a positive write-up about him in their Association's *Northwest Sports Angler* magazine. Apparently when the February issue came out a few weeks ago, it wasn't in there. Abel was telling him he was going to turn the letter over to the commercials. Curtin was, essentially pleading with him not to do that. From the look on Curtin's face when he left, well, if you were looking for a likely culprit…"

"So, when Abel didn't turn the letter over to us, you decided to do it yourself."

She took a deep breath. "I know, Sandy. But I'd really had it with him, by then. You guys needed that letter. It was time Abel stopped playing games. That thing was forwarded to him. Whoever did that expected him to give it to you. Maybe, sooner or later, they'd have found another way to do that themselves. Meanwhile, that damned initiative has been filed. They're out getting signatures, seeking endorsements, raising money." Judith paused for a moment. "You know this wasn't the first time he'd done this kind of thing. That business with holding up your gillnet/birds bill in rules, that's the same kind of thing. It's just an abuse of power."

I certainly agreed with her on that. "At least that wasn't blackmail. Not like this thing you're describing with Curtin."

"Well, it wasn't the first time he'd done that either."

I just gave her a questioning look.

"I'm only saying, he was doing the exact same damn thing to that nice young man that works for the Northwest Tribal Fisheries Consortium. Doing it for you, I might add"

"For me?" Now I was puzzled. "Are you talking about Jerry Stockmeyer?"

"Yeah, Stockmeyer, and yes, for you—for your clients. You know, you may be feeling all 'hard done to' with this initiative from Clive Curtin and his buddies. But, you're not above some deception yourself, Sandy. You remember last year when the sportsmen showed up and killed your clever little 'catch all the non-Tribal share' bill, the one that would have required the Department to maximize the non-tribal salmon catch?"

I did recall. I'd had a good thing going with that bill until the sportsmen figured it out at the last minute and came in and killed it.

I had to confess that she might have a point about it having been deceptive. At least if you ignored the context.

The Indian Tribes in the Pacific Northwest had federal treaties that guaranteed them at least fifty-percent of the catch of salmon passing through each of their "usual and accustomed fishing grounds." In practice, that meant they actually caught more than just fifty percent because the Tribes' "usual and accustomed fishing grounds" were frequently in the individual streams and rivers where the fish go to spawn. Traditional non-tribal fisheries took place out at sea or in large salt-water estuaries like Puget Sound where the many runs from all those rivers and streams are mixed together. That meant the non-Tribal fisheries had to stop when all the available harvest of fish from the weakest of those runs had been taken. Tribal members fishing the streams where the runs were still healthy and strong could continue to fish, and, as a result, they ended up catching more than half the fish available for harvest.

What really aggravated my clients was when the Department of Fish and Wildlife cut commercial fisheries short so anglers would have greater "fishing opportunity." In order to provide truly good fishing for sportsmen, there needed to be a lot of fish present while they were fishing. It meant that far more fish had to be left uncaught by the commercial fleet and be made available in the sport fishery so the anglers, with their recreational hook and line gear, could actually catch some. A great many of those extra fish ended up swimming safely on past the anglers and were ultimately caught by in-stream Tribal fishermen, yet further increasing their catch beyond their legally-mandated fifty-percent minimum.

This was a double insult because most of the discussion of all this happened behind closed doors between "sovereigns"—the State and the Tribes. No Open Public Meetings Law applied.

My bill would have ended this practice. It had simply required that, insofar as was fully consistent with lawful Tribal treaty fishing rights, non-tribal fisheries should be managed so they caught as much as legally possible of their remaining share. To comply, the Fisheries Department would have had to maximize sustainable harvests on the stronger runs of salmon. That would have ended what we considered to be the Department's "extra-legal" dabbling in sport priority.

"I bet you're wondering how the sports guys caught on to what that bill was really all about," Judith prompted my thoughts.

I nodded. That caught my attention. Until now, I'd believed they'd just figured it out by themselves.

"Well, the person that tipped them off was Jerry Stockmeyer."

"Really?" Stockmeyer was the Tribes' government relations guy; he lobbied for them in the State Legislature. "He and I talked about it beforehand," I said. "He told me himself the Tribes wouldn't take a position on it."

Judith shook her head. "Sandy, come on. You know that bill was going to reduce the actual Tribal catch, even if it didn't affect their treaty-protected rights."

"Yeah, of course. But, the Tribes stay scrupulously out of anything dealing with the non-Tribal share. They know how that would look; they wouldn't have done it. Jerry wouldn't have done it either. His bosses would have been angry as hell if that became public."

She smiled. "Yeah, but he did. I think he was just irritated by the duplicity of it. You know full well that a lot of these elected legislators hate the Indian Treaties even though they can't do anything about them. The idea that non-tribal fishermen might be prevented from catching their full fifty-percent share is abhorrent. Those sportsmen think the same thing: why should the Tribes be catching more than their half? Most of them aren't all that savvy about the complications of harvest management, or of the Treaties. You know full well you were trying to slip that bill by them; same as they're trying to do now on this ballot initiative. Jerry was bothered by it. He sent them an anonymous letter."

"I'll be damned." Jerry Stockmeyer had more nerve than I'd given him credit for. "Still, what does this have to do with Abel?"

"Abel caught him at it. Or... I guess more accurately, I did," she admitted.

"You did?"

"He was in here for a meeting with the Senator last year, a day or two before that hearing on your bill. When he left, he forgot his little computer, left it sitting on that chair. When I picked it up and put it on my desk, the screen lit up; it was still on, and there, big as life, was the letter he'd written to Clive Curtin explaining how your bill was going to screw the sportsmen. He must have been reading it and laid it down and forgot it when he went in to meet the Senator. I showed it to the Senator and he took a picture of it with his phone. Then we just shut it down. I was about to call up Stockmeyer's office when he showed up back here and picked it up."

While I was surprised, I wasn't necessarily all that angry to learn what Jerry Stockmeyer had done. I couldn't truthfully say I might not have done the same thing in his position. "If his bosses knew he'd done that, they'd be very angry."

"Of course. If it became public, it would have been deeply embarrassing for the Tribes to be caught playing politics behind the scenes with the non-tribal catch. The Senator knew that. He brought Stockmeyer in here, a week or so ago, and used that letter to twist his arm into getting the Tribes to oppose the sportsmen's initiative."

"I'll be damned!" I doubted the Tribes would ever actually take such a position. If you thought about it, they'd benefit if it passed. Although they might see that as a strong reason to stay out of it— to not be seen as meddling in non-tribal affairs. But, it was at least interesting to know that Mortenson had been trying to help. The manipulative son-of-a-bitch couldn't stay on the sidelines of anything. He'd been trying to cozy up to the sportsmen but, at the same time, here he was working against them on their beloved ballot initiative. It all just confirmed my suspicion that he was a classic passive-aggressive. It probably didn't matter to him who the target was, or what the issue. He just enjoyed seeing people squirm.

In my mind, I began piecing together what I feared might be a challenging conversation with Jerry Stockmeyer.

Then another question occurred to me: "How much of this did you mention to the State Patrol," I asked.

"Not much that first day," she said. "I was pretty shaken up. I made a 'statement' for one of the officers before they sent me home. But none of this stuff even came up."

"But, afterward…?"

"Yeah, well, the next day, on Tuesday, that Lieutenant Wilson came by. By then I'd given it some thought. He asked me what I knew about Clive Curtin's dealings with the Senator. I told him about that letter Curtin had written and how the Senator had been holding him up with it. I'm sure Curtin had nothing to do with this. But, well, it seemed like something the Lieutenant should know. By then I'd already given it to Stephanie to give to you anyway."

"And Jerry? You mention this thing with Jerry Stockmeyer and my bill last year?"

"Yeah, that too. Once I'd mentioned Curtin's letter, well, that thing with Stockmeyer and your bill seemed like something I ought to mention too. I mean, it was basically the same kind of thing, you know."

I did. I was impressed to learn that Wilson was delving into some of this. And pleased to learn he was considering other suspects. At least I wasn't alone.

"Judith, you've been fiercely loyal to Senator Mortenson for years. What happened to change all that?" I asked. "What did the Senator do that made you angry enough to do this?"

"I'd just had it with him, that's all. Had enough of his games and playing people off against each other."

"But he's always done that. It's who he was."

"I know, Sandy. I know. I'd just had enough."

I pressed, but Judith closed down. There was nothing more she was going to say.

Chapter Ten

Thursday, March 4, 2:15 p.m.

A Return to the Order of Business

I left Judith clearing out the Senator's files and headed back up the street to my office. A lot of work had accumulated over the past few days while I'd been distracted by Senator Mortenson's unsettling death. It was only by pure chance that, later that same day, I happened upon what might have been the real reason for Judith Bosch's aggravation with her boss.

There was a privately-owned but largely abandoned street-end in Gig Harbor that was used by my fishermen clients as a launching ramp for their boats. It was also put to the same use by a good many sportsmen and recreational boaters. All of them had been startled to discover it wasn't public land when a fence and a "for sale" sign had suddenly appeared one day last year. Later, faced with community pressure, the owner had ultimately agreed to take the property off the market and to submit it, instead, to the Washington Wildlife and Recreation Program. That's the program that, in our state, prioritizes State purchases of land for public environmental and recreational purposes. The launching ramp property was now on the WWRP acquisitions list where candidates for such land purchases are prioritized from most desirable to least in the appropriation for that purpose. I was wondering where my clients' launch site stood and looked it up on the "Access Washington" website.

That's where I noticed that the Piet Bosch Dairy of Lynden, WA, was on the WWRP farmland easement list.

I remembered Stephanie Miles mentioning that Judith's aging

father was a big worry for her. He apparently refused to sell out and retire. This was not uncommon. Older farmers, like Piet Bosch, often resisted giving up their farms because the only people who could afford to buy them were developers. Many times, they'd been born on their land and then inherited it from their farming families. They'd spend a lifetime of living and working on a property, struggling to improve the soil, refine drainage and irrigation, plant the best crops, build the right fences, improve the barns and work-buildings, and otherwise make it into the perfect farm. So, it wasn't surprising when they simply couldn't face the prospect of their multi-generational family farm being finally turned into some ugly housing development or paved over as parking for a strip mall.

A lot of my fishermen clients doubled as farmers. I knew that dairying was an especially tough business. There were all kinds of normal risks like sick cows, bad weather, and spikes in the cost of feed. The price of milk was notorious for dramatic, unpredictable fluctuations. Small dairy farmers, like Judith's dad, kept incredibly long hours and were tied to their operations year-round by the never-ending needs of their livestock. A lot of them couldn't take vacations.

The kicker was the rising cost of land. The old days, when a typical, dairy was 100 cows on 100 acres, were long gone. Now it was all about consolidation. The price of flat, fertile, healthy pasture had skyrocketed. It was no longer possible for a single cow to support the ownership of an acre of land. Instead, the modern dairy might easily have 2,000 cows on fifty acres—something like forty cows per acre.

One cow per acre was generally considered environmentally sustainable. The new trend toward consolidation had ended the old, traditional model in which the cows grew healthy on grasses that had been fertilized by their own manure. These days, they ate grain and hay purchased and hauled in from elsewhere. Their waste was stored in huge lagoons for later removal and discharge elsewhere. That involved a big investment in animals and in the equipment and infrastructure to support them. It involved new, complicated waste management storage and treatment systems. It required new, hired labor.

The economics of consolidation worked, particularly in reducing the business cost of owning land. But cash poor, small scale, traditional family dairy farmers like Piet Bosch often couldn't afford it. They now had to compete with all these new, efficient, industrial dairies. They often struggled along hand-to-mouth until age or illness caught up. Then they were forced to sell to fund their retirement. The buyer would typically be a developer. They'd watch their treasured family homestead, the focus of a lifetime of dreams and labor, get covered up by a golf course, suburban homes, strip malls, or condominiums.

WWRP's farmland conservation program was designed to help local counties and land trusts purchase a protective easement on working farms to prevent them from being developed. The farmer would receive the difference in value between what a developer might pay and what another farmer could afford. The land could then be sold to another farmer and would stay in agriculture. The elderly farmer could then retire with fair compensation, a happy heart, and a clean conscience.

Unfortunately, the Piet Bosch dairy was fairly well down on the WWRP priority lists. Its inclusion in this year's budget was in serious doubt. WWRP was popular and had purchased well-loved lands in every community in the state. It had support from a strong coalition of hunters, fishermen, and environmentalists. Usually, the WWRP battle went to the urban liberals. In a usual Legislative Session, the Piet Bosch Dairy would have been included.

But, conservatives and budget hawks hated it. This year, if the Republicans got their way, they were going to cut that budget in half. Up until a few days ago, that had seemed likely. But now, with the 'Ds' in charge, all that could change.

On a chance, I phoned Stephanie Miles's office and caught her on the way to a meeting. "Oh yeah," she said. "Judith's dad's dairy is definitely on the WWRP list. Judith is really hopeful. If it gets funded, it's going to make a lot of difference to her and her family."

"Any chance you know what position Senator Mortenson took on the matter," I asked.

"Huh? No. No idea," she replied.

It wasn't much of a leap, however, to guess. In cementing his ties to his conservative Republican cohorts, Mortenson would have supported their tightly restrictive budget appropriation for WWRP. Many Republicans and even a few conservative Democrats like Mortenson, believed land should be privately owned and freely traded on the private economy. Of course, I very much doubted Mortenson would have had strong, personal, principled feelings on the matter.

But he was all for making policy choices that served his personal self-interest. He liked the power he'd been given by his Republican cohorts. I was sure he'd have been very slow to put that at risk by crossing them on something like this.

On the other hand, this *was* something he *could* have influenced—if he'd wanted to. And I felt confident Judith knew that. She definitely would have raised it with him.

He obviously hadn't exercised that influence, because, at least as of Monday, the Republican budget position on WWRP hadn't changed. Judith might have been very angry about that. It could explain why she'd suddenly started working at cross-purposes with her boss after all these years. And, perhaps, why she'd been so reticent to mention it to me.

I had to admit, it was hard to see Judith as a killer. Sure, it was possible she'd waited in the ladies' room, come back to the office after I'd left, killed the Senator, and then gone blithely out to lunch with friends. Or, given that the coroner couldn't pin down the time of the murder, she could have done it immediately when she'd returned, and then just enacted her theatrical "finding a body" scene for the benefit of witnesses.

Maybe there were depths to Judith Bosch that weren't obvious.

Neither of those possibilities seemed likely. That being said, I was seriously troubled that she had been less than forthcoming about the WWRP matter.

Chapter Eleven

Friday March 5, 10:00 a.m.

Reaching Out to an Ally

The offices of the Northwest Tribal Fisheries Consortium were in downtown Olympia, several blocks south of the Capitol. They were on the third floor of a modern office building near the waterfront. When I arrived, their receptionist showed me into a large conference room just off their reception area. The room had a nice view north up the West Bay and out onto South Puget Sound. Appropriate, I thought, for an organization that led the ongoing fight for the legal rights of its member Tribes to fish those waters and managed the resulting tribal fisheries there.

The Northwest's Indian Tribes were, unquestionably, the people with the most reason to care about the region's salmon. They'd depended on salmon eons before any European laid eyes on the North American continent. Salmon were integral to their culture. Even with the new casinos, fishing was still the Tribes' economic bedrock. And the Tribes' future was, in many respects, also legally bound to the future of salmon by their Treaties with the Federal Government. Those treaties had first been signed back in the 1850s, but they had been largely ignored until 1974 when a wise and fearless Federal District Court Judge by the name of George Boldt had finally ruled that Tribal fishermen were entitled to half the total catch.

The resulting shift in harvest was tectonic for both Tribal and non-tribal fishermen. The Boldt Decision produced a major (and much needed) economic boost for the Tribes. But many non-Indian fishermen found the losses in non-Tribal fisheries hard to accept.

Resentments from the decision continued to this day.

Mounted on the walls around the NTFC conference room where I sat waiting were several old framed photographs of people I recognized, pictures taken in the 1960s and 1970s. Most were news shots of much younger versions of current, highly-respected Tribal leaders engaged in what had, at the time, been "illegal" fishing during their political protests prior to and following the Boldt Decision. Until the U.S. Supreme Court finally settled the matter by affirming Boldt's ruling, the Pacific Northwest had experienced several years of legal fights, protests, sabotage, and even some violence. Many of the Tribal members who had participated in those protests, and whose pictures were on that wall, were now respected board members in the NTFC. The fight for Tribal fishing rights had been a Pacific Northwest parallel to the civil rights movement. And the proud display of their pictures in that Conference room made it perfectly clear that this was exactly how these Tribal leaders had seen their role at that time and how they still saw it today.

Having finally won those rights, they were *never* going to allow them to be lost again.

I was fond of Jerry Stockmeyer. He was an Eastern transplant whose Jersey boy accent and the accompanying attitude still sometimes bled through despite his years in the Pacific Northwest. He was also a complete professional, an unabashed environmentalist, and a true-believer in the Tribal cause. Jerry's mom, who, I understood, had been his large family's sole support, had driven a transit bus in Newark. But Jerry had been a sufficient prodigy to win a scholarship to Princeton. After graduating in marine biology, he'd come west for a Masters in fisheries at the University of Washington, after which he'd gone to work with NTFC's harvest management staff. I'd dealt with him on several previous occasions even before last year when they'd promoted him to be their Government Affairs Director. Before that, he'd been a frequent technical participant for NTFC at the annual Pacific Fisheries Management Council process. That was where the western states, Tribes, and Federal government met annually to set the basic regulatory framework for the region's salmon harvest. He'd also been a frequent Tribal witness on technical harvest management issues in legislative hearings. So, from time to time, we'd met on the hill as well.

Jerry's new job lobbying for Indian Tribes in a state legislature couldn't have been an easy one. Especially for someone with his technical background. The job was doubly difficult because not everyone understood the Tribes' unique status under U.S. law. By treaty, the Tribes were sovereign powers. Their members were citizens of their respective tribal nations. At the same time, they were also citizens of the United States, and of their state of residence. They voted in elections like everybody else. They ran for public office. They attended public schools. They held jobs. And they served, scrupulously, faithfully, and almost to a man, in the U.S. military. Until you understood that dual role, it was hard to appreciate their point of view.

As long as non-Tribal commercial fishermen respected their legal fishing rights, the Tribes' interest in the salmon harvest was generally consistent with ours—mine and my clients, that is. It was the Department of Fish & Wildlife that we didn't really trust. And, now that the Boldt Decision was largely implemented and accepted, it was the sportsmen who were our usual source of grief.

Of course, a great many legislators were deeply ambivalent about the Tribes. They, like many of their non-tribal constituents, often still resented the Tribes' unique legal status or were simply ignorant of what it involved. Sadly, among those legislators who *did* understand, there were some for whom, the better they understood, the more trouble they caused.

Abel Mortenson's district had a significant Tribal presence. And he'd occasionally come down on the Tribes' side. In fact, the knife that had killed him had been presented as a gift from one of the Tribes in his district in appreciation for his help on one of those rare occasions. But his priorities were never clear. Whoever could help him stay elected usually came first. Tribes weren't exactly out of the running, but they didn't represent a sufficiently large voting block to be decisive. And there were some issues on which they were at odds with non-tribal constituents whose votes he badly needed. Mortenson had been entirely capable of flagrant pandering to his constituents' baser anti-Tribal sentiments when the occasion presented itself. Dealing with him had to have been frustrating for Jerry Stockmeyer.

Jerry joined me in the conference room. He was a bit surprised. "To what do I owe the pleasure?" he asked, taking off his wire rimmed glasses. It looked like I'd pulled him away from some kind of detail work.

"Well, it's not so much for pleasure, actually, Jerry." I looked around.

The conference room door was still wide open. There was a large interior window that opened onto the entry area where people were standing and talking and others were coming and going just outside the door. It seemed awfully public. "Um, do you have an office?"

"Sure, Sandy." Jerry was something of a technocrat, with the kind of focused skills that had always escaped me but that I could definitely respect. He led the way back down the hall to his cluttered office, removed some old reports from a chair for me, and closed the door before sitting behind his desk. "What's this all about?"

I couldn't see any way to start but at the beginning. "Remember that bill I had last year, the one that would have required the Department to maximize the non-tribal harvest share?"

"Yeah. I remember," Jerry said guardedly.

"Well… I learned earlier today that it was you who tipped off Curtin and his guys about how that bill would affect the sports fisheries. Senator Mortenson's L.A. told me about it."

"She did?" He looked decidedly chagrined.

I held up my hand and did my best at a friendly smile. "Look, Jerry, you need to know I don't really fault you for that. I might have done the same thing, in your position. I wouldn't even mention it to you, but some things have come up and I need to talk with you about it. I hope that's okay."

I think Jerry Stockmeyer was blushing. After a moment's hesitation, he made an obvious decision to come clean. "I'm really sorry about that, Sandy," he said with a sigh. "I hope you know I would never have done that if the thing hadn't had an impact on the Tribal catch. It just seemed wrong that the Tribes' determination to maintain good relationships with the non-tribal community would cost them fish, at least in this particular way."

"No problem. It's history, Jerry. I assume you know I proposed that bill because my clients are being screwed over by the sports-biased managers at the Department. That's also wrong, in my opinion. I think, maybe more than anyone, you'll understand exactly what I mean."

"I guess I do."

"After several years of sport priority bullshit from Curtin and his guys, I confess, I also just wanted to stick it to them once in return. Maybe I *should* feel guilty about it. But I don't. Anyway, I don't see why anybody needs to know about your anonymous letter. As far as I'm concerned, it never happened. And I'm definitely not here to challenge you about it."

"Thanks, Sandy. I appreciate that. I probably shouldn't have done it." He nodded his head toward his office door. "And these guys could be deeply embarrassed if it ever became public that I had. They don't deserve that."

"Worry not." Then, trying for a change of subject: "I just mention it because, well… I had a visit from the State Patrol the other day. I was Senator Mortenson's last appointment just before he was killed on Monday. We argued over a little stunt he was pulling, holding up one of my bills solely because he was mad about something I wrote in the WCSC Newsletter."

"The State Patrol? What do they have to do with this?"

"They apparently have jurisdiction over crimes on the Capitol Campus."

"Huh. A bit of a reach from traffic tickets."

"It does seem that way. Um, anyway, look, Mortenson's LA, Judith, told me something else as well. I'm just going to be up front about it. She says Mortenson wanted you to get the Consortium Tribes to oppose this Salmon Protection Act ballot measure. That he threatened you with making your anonymous letter on my bill public."

That obviously put Stockmeyer back on his heels. He took a moment. Then he breathed deeply, and said: "You know, that man represented everything I hate about this job." He gave me his tired smile. "Salmon resource is going to hell. But all he could ever think about was his own damn political self-interest. He never did a thing that didn't somehow work to his own personal benefit."

"What did you tell him?"

"I told him no."

"You have to have been tempted to try."

"Of course, I was," Jerry said. "But I couldn't do that even if I'd wanted to. Which I didn't. The leadership here makes those kinds of decisions. And there's no way on earth they'll take a position on that initiative. Even if I thought they should do it, and I don't, it's established policy. Just wasn't in my power to accomplish."

"What would have happened if Mortenson had made good on his threat—passed your letter along to your bosses or made it public?" I asked.

"I'd have probably been fired. At least disciplined. You know what would happen if it became generally known that the Tribes had interfered in a non-Tribal harvest allocation matter. There'd have been hell to pay. Your guys would have raised hell. Half the Legislature would have been up in arms. The Tribes could kiss good-bye to the friendly, collegial relationships they've fought to nurture over the past thirty years. It would seriously damage our carefully developed public narrative that the Indian Tribes want to be good neighbors and reliable partners now and for generations to come."

"What was Mortenson going to do?"

"I have no idea. When he died, I figured maybe it was over. I've got to admit, you're not bringing welcome news. I hope you mean what you say about keeping it quiet."

"I do. It could come out anyway. But, as far as I'm concerned, there's no need for anyone to know... unless, of course you killed him to keep it that way." I did my best to say it lightly, like a joke. I did want to see Stockmeyer's reaction. Maybe the killer had chosen that Lummi ceremonial knife purposely out of some kind of symbolic irony.

"Oh, Christ, I hope you don't think that, Sandy."

"No, I don't. But it's not impossible you could be asked by the Patrol about your letter and about where you were on Monday over lunch."

Stockmeyer paused a moment, thinking that over. "I don't know. Um, it seems like I bought something to-go from the little deli, downstairs. Ate here in my office. Was back up on the hill in the afternoon."

"You might be thinking about who saw you here."

"I doubt anybody did, at least not that would remember. Maybe the receptionist, but I doubt it. And, anyway, there's a back stairway right out here at the end of the hall."

"That puts you and me in the same position. I was in his office just before it happened. Went back to my office right after our meeting. But, as far as I know, nobody can testify to that either."

Jerry Stockmeyer shook his head with a wry laugh. "Well, I guess I can understand why you're asking questions. Like you, I'd much prefer staying out of jail."

"Well I have still another one. Both of us had occasion to watch Abel Mortenson at work. We both know, full well, what he was like. Is there anybody else you know of that I should talk to? Maybe someone who might have had it in for the good Senator?"

It was obvious immediately that Stockmeyer had an answer. But he was hesitating.

Perhaps he needed some prompting: "You know, Jerry, the last thing in the world I wanted to do was come here today and ask you all these questions. But we live in a tight little world here. I think there's a good chance whoever killed the Senator will turn out to be someone we both know. Maybe even someone we like. I've got too much at stake to let that stop me. I think we both do. If you have some thoughts, you need to let me know."

Now Stockmeyer said. "Well, it's about Martin Rose. I assume, you like and respect Martin as I do. We're occasionally at odds, but I don't, for a moment, think he'd do something like this. He did have something strange going on with the Senator, however. Just like me."

"Hmm." I knew Martin Rose well. He was the Legislative Liaison for the Department of Fish and Wildlife so we worked together all of the time.

"You know the Tribes and the Department often collaborate on salmon habitat stuff?"

"Of course."

"Martin and I had lunch together just yesterday. We're working on an appropriation for culvert improvements that eliminate fish passage barriers. Martin mentioned this letter. It was an email message that had originated with Clive Curtin spelling out the sportsmen's strategy behind their 'Salmon Protection Act' ballot initiative. Maybe you already know about it?"

"Yeah, I think I do."

"Well, Mortenson apparently showed that letter to Martin. Twisted Martin's arm to get *him* to give it to you guys without getting Mortenson involved. Guess he figured if Martin did it, he'd never dare admit it. Martin was worried about it, he needed to keep the Department out of it. On Monday everything changed. He can forget about it now, especially since you apparently already have the thing."

Amazing. there it was again—Abel freaking Mortenson! The man was a case.

A few minutes later I was on my way back up to the Capitol. As I walked, I considered what Jerry Stockmeyer had said. It was hard to conceive of him as a killer. But, it did strike me that he hadn't ever actually denied having murdered Senator Abel Mortenson.

His job was certainly a lot more secure now, with the Senator dead.

Chapter Twelve

Friday, March 5, 4:00 p.m.

A Strategic Sidebar

I t was still cool but sunny late that Friday afternoon when I called Martin Rose and then caught up with him as he was leaving the Capital Building. I joined him in his walk back down to his office in the Natural Resources Building, five or ten minutes away. The route was a pleasant one. It passed the impressive bronze World War II memorial with its "Winged Victory" statue and the Tivoli Fountain. All of it was on paved walks across a broad expanse of carefully tended lawn before crossing Capitol way and heading downhill into a complex of buildings occupied by the State's various administrative agencies.

It was the perfect opportunity for a pleasant but private conversation.

Martin Rose was as much a fixture at the State Capitol as Mortenson had been, though a much more congenial one. There had been times, in years past, when the sport-commercial battles had placed my clients at odds with the Department. I believed this was for no more complicated reason than that Olympia, a relatively small town, was itself on the shores of Puget Sound. Many of the agency's full-time professional office staff were anglers themselves and, for that reason, simply found the sportsmen's case more sympathetic. I'd always found Martin to be savvy, prudent, and reasonable. More often than not we'd ended up on the same side, if for no other reason than that my clients and I were usually in the right.

I considered him more than just a colleague, and I wanted to keep it that way.

"Earlier this week," I told him when we joined up, "we got an interesting letter. It was written back in November by Clive Curtin to his sports allies. It rather nicely explains the rationale for their ballot initiative."

"Did you?"

"We did. Maybe you might like me to send you a copy... if you haven't already seen it, of course."

"You think I might have seen it?"

"Well, if you have, and if you were wondering about passing it along to us, I thought you might like to know we already have it... so you needn't bother."

That succeeded in raising his eyebrows. "Well," he said. "If I'd seen such a letter, I'm sure you know I'd let you know about it right away." He was smiling.

I smiled back: "Wouldn't doubt it for a minute."

"It is nice that you mention it, Sandy. If I had seen it, you'd have saved me the trouble of sending it over."

I had to grin. The man was sometimes just a joy to be around. He and I both knew that for him to be seen passing along to us information that might be politically useful in our fight against the anglers' ballot initiative could compromise his and the Department's carefully guarded "impartiality" in the sports-commercial conflict.

"Would you like *me* to send *you* a copy? It's a doozy," I said.

"No, don't bother. I think I already have a pretty good idea what it says."

With that out of the way, I knew Jerry Stockmeyer had been right about Mortenson twisting Martin's arm over Clive Curtin's letter. That was almost certainly how Martin already knew about that letter's existence.

For a few moments, we walked along together in companionable silence. I was quite aware that he might be sensitive on the matters I wanted to discuss. Most of us that worked at the Capitol knew that Martin was on thin ice with his bosses at the moment.

I'd been in the room, a couple of weeks earlier, when he'd testified in the House Natural Resources Committee on an obnoxious bill sponsored by Representative Tony Underhill. Underhill was from Goldendale, down near the Columbia River. He earned most of his living as a public relations consultant to the hydropower industry. Underhill's clients were the agencies that operated dams on the Columbia. And most of his constituents were farmers who were fed up with environmental regulations that cost them a lot of money in the name of protecting wild endangered salmon. Like his constituents, Underhill didn't care a whit about protecting salmon. He was interested in protecting the irrigation water, the cheap energy, and the jobs produced by those dams.

"So, Mr. Rose," Underhill had asked when Martin had completed his prepared statement at that hearing on the bill. "You're saying it isn't possible for fishermen to catch hatchery salmon without also catching some wild salmon that come from runs which are endangered and which may even be listed under the Endangered Species Act?"

"That's right. Of course, as I'm sure you know, all our fisheries, sport and commercial, are quite selective. We greatly minimize any impact on endangered runs."

"Even so, some endangered fish are inevitably taken, right?"

"Yes sir, that is correct."

"So, if any one of us in this room today, anyone at all, were to walk into a seafood restaurant, a fish market, or a grocery store and buy a salmon for dinner, there's every real possibility, without knowing the difference, that we could end up eating a fish that was actually listed under the Endangered Species Act?"

"That would be extraordinarily unlikely. But, yes, it's possible."

"Well then, Mr. Rose, what I fail to understand is why the public agency of our State responsible for protecting those endangered fish wouldn't support legislation to end all fishing for salmon that causes mortality in endangered runs until such time as those runs recover."

Martin was a very careful and savvy guy. Even from the back of the room, however, I could tell by his stiffening posture that Underhill's terminal stupidity was eroding his better judgment. That's when he screwed up.

"Mr. Chairman," Martin said. "Perhaps the Representative might entertain a simple, friendly amendment to the proposed legislation."

"And what would that be, Mr. Rose?" asked Underhill.

"Given the Representative's concern for these endangered fish, I believe a minor change in the wording might make the bill much more effective at achieving its stated purposes. Let me draw your attention to page 2 at line 18, where it reads: '...prohibit all sport and commercial fisheries that result in incidental harm to salmon runs listed as threatened or endangered under the Federal Endangered Species Act...' " Martin pointedly waited a moment, and then continued: "Perhaps we might simply delete the words: 'sport and commercial fisheries' and replace them with the words: 'human activities.' I'm quite sure such a change would, at the very least, cause the Department to take another look at its current position on the bill."

There was a momentary rustle of paper as Committee Members turned to the appropriate page and line in their briefing books and as the lobbyists, activists, and constituents around me in the audience shuffled through their copies of the bill. Then there were a few muffled but unmistakable snickers. Grins, some more subdued than others, appeared on several of the faces of the other Committee Members as they came to understand how this mockingly-suggested amendment would completely eliminate all hydropower, agriculture, construction, aerospace, and a great many, maybe most, other current industries and activities in the State of Washington. Nothing of the kind, of course, would ever pass.

Representative Underhill was furious. "I have no further need of you, Mr. Rose," he said. He was seething. As the Chair called the next witness and Martin stood to head back down the aisle toward the door, I could tell by his reaction to the succession of smiles, nods, and occasional subtly whispered "way to goes" that he was well aware he'd just made a very big mistake. In the moment, his very public, implied suggestion for where Underhill could take his stupid bill and stick it had, no doubt, felt quite good. Everyone knew Underhill's bill for what it was: a politician pandering to his constituents. And a sop for Underhill's valued consulting clients in the hydropower community, clients whose dams killed far more endangered salmon than any other activity in the Pacific Northwest.

Martin should probably have just remained silent. The bill was never going to pass. So there'd been no need for him to stand up to Underhill like that. Representative Underhill was clueless and pig-headed, but he was also popular with his constituents and secure in his seat. With the current Republican hegemony in the Senate, Underhill was also influential. No doubt Underhill would speak to Fisheries Director Prince. It was a virtual certainty that Martin would be called in to talk with his boss before the day was out. Martin had just made a serious enemy. His boss wouldn't like it.

A couple of days later, I'd run into Martin at the Republican entrance to the Senate Chamber in the Capitol Rotunda. He had, indeed, been called in for a dressing down. But, when he got home that evening, his wife, unlike Director Prince, thought what he'd done was the funniest thing she'd ever heard. She was, herself, a State employee, a program manager over in the Transportation Department, and knew a good deal about the inner workings of State Agencies. She'd asked him if Prince had put him on probation, issued a letter of caution, or taken any other official action. Martin had been forced to tell her no, none of that had happened. Then she'd bet him a crab dinner at Gardner's in Olympia, that, at that very moment, Prince was home with *his* wife and they were cracking up about it as well.

I had to admit, that seemed entirely possible to me. But Martin, a serious guy, was very much on edge and feeling the need to tread carefully.

I too, needed to use care.

"Well, it looks like a clean slate over in the Senate," I said, opening up a new line of conversation. The Democrats had caucused and then called the Senate into Session the day before. The Lieutenant Governor was a Democrat and even without Mortenson's replacement yet in place, Republican control of the process had already shifted. Several bills that were through Rules but hadn't yet been scheduled for the floor were back in limbo. The 'Ds' had appointed an entirely new slate of committee chairs. They'd pushed back the cutoff calendar a few days. All previously scheduled committee meetings were being rescheduled. The new chairs were starting over from scratch with a fresh hearings calendar. A lot of stuff was going to fall by the wayside and I was betting that some bills that had died would come to life.

"They move fast when they have to, I guess," he said.

"Interesting times."

"I'll say."

"I'm not sure where we're going to be without him. I assume the 'Ds' have replaced him on the Committee with Jimmy Fang?" I asked.

"Yep."

"I think we're still okay with Senator Fang. But I've definitely got some catching up to do." Fortunately, the Department had opposed the current sport priority bill. They could be counted on to generally oppose anything that constrained the Director's authority to manage the fisheries. A ballot initiative, of course, was another matter entirely.

We'd entered the large, open lobby of the Natural Resources Building. There was a lot of end-of-day traffic exiting the down elevator cars. But Martin and I caught an empty on the way back up.

"Well, it's nice having company on my walk, Sandy. But, how can I be of service?"

I needed to get to the point. I smiled and sallied forth: "Well, I'm a little worried to find myself something of a suspect in all this. I've been talking to a few people, seeing what I can learn."

"Ah. Conducting something of an 'independent' investigation, you could say."

"Well, maybe more like a few casual questions. See what turns up."

On the 6th floor, we fell silent as Martin led me down the hall and then through a warren of now mostly-empty cubicles to his office that, unlike most State employee workspaces, thankfully had an actual door.

"Have the State Patrol guys spoken to you?" I asked as Martin hung up his coat and sat behind his desk.

"Not as yet. I suppose they'll get around to it. When they do, I'll be glad to put in a good word on your behalf."

I smiled at that. "They have a Lieutenant Wilson working the case. Heads a General Investigations Unit."

"An administrator? Handling an on-the-ground investigation? Not a detective?"

"I wondered the same thing. You think that's unusual?"

"Not sure. Maybe," he said.

I didn't know how to go about getting what I needed without just asking. So I went for it. "I assume they don't know Mortenson was twisting your arm to turn Clive Curtin's letter over to us?"

That drew a sharp glance. And then: "I guess you've been talking with Jerry Stockmeyer."

"In Jerry's defense, I pressured him some. He speaks very highly of you, by the way."

"He should. I've been mentoring him for the past year. He's turning out well, I'd say."

"What did you tell Mortenson?"

"I told him I'd do it. But I was just buying time. Even if I didn't get caught, Mortenson might still have seen fit to mention it later to my boss. Or he might have just held me up with it. If he'd told Director

Prince, I'd have been out of a job for sure. Of course, Mortenson could have screwed me anyway, if he'd wanted. Over the years, I've just done what I needed to do to keep him sweet. This was a bit different. If I got the Department publicly in the middle of a political fight on some ballot initiative, they'd be one-hundred percent in the right to let me go."

"I have to admit, I've wondered sometimes how someone like Mortenson comes to think they can just get away with that kind of stuff, without consequences."

"Actually, all those people over there," he aimed a thumb in the direction of the Capitol Building, "the 'electeds.' They all live in a bubble. Mortenson was a bad case. But it goes with the job, even for the ones that seem normal."

"Yeah," I said. "Maybe you're right."

"You know, I once ran for public office."

"Really?" I hadn't known that.

"For Congress in the Ninth District. At the time, that covered the area south of Seattle and included some of Tacoma. Ran as a moderate Republican," he smiled, "back when there was such a thing. Made a serious bid. Lost in the primary, but it was a close call. Had a whole, big, complicated campaign. Half a dozen paid staffers plus a campaign consultant and, at the end, maybe twenty or thirty volunteers working the phones. Had someone keeping my calendar. Someone driving me everywhere. Someone would brief me before and after each fund-raiser, interview, and speaking event. Wherever I went, whatever I did, all day there were people there asking my opinion, filming or recording what I said, and helping me figure out what to do and say next. The night of the primary, we had close to 150 people there at the campaign office, staff, friends, supporters, even some press. Big deal."

He was shaking his head at the recollection. "We'd rented this big open storefront in a mall along Highway 99. The morning after the loss, my wife and I showed up at the office about nine or so. Of course, the place was empty. No staff. No volunteers. No press. All gone. Just us. Place was a tomb. And it was a big mess from the night before. I recall standing there, looking around, and noticing all the litter on the floor. And I remember thinking: 'Huh! Damn! I guess if that stuff is going to get picked up, it's *me* that's going to have to do it.' I'd only been involved in the campaign for maybe six months. But, somehow that came as a really big surprise."

Martin glanced at the clock on his wall. It was getting late. I did have another question. "Lieutenant Wilson wanted to know where I was over lunch on Monday," I said.

Martin smiled and nodded. "I'm sure he did. And that was...?"

"Alone, back in my office. No real alibi."

"I gather you'd like to know where *I* might have been during that time?"

"Well, yeah... I would, Martin."

He gave it some thought. "I'm afraid, at least for most of it, I was in the back corner of the Coffee Shop in the basement of the Capitol Building. Eating a large white chocolate chip cookie and drinking coffee. My lunch, such as it was. I was reading some bill reports. Made a few calls, but that could have been from anywhere. I saw a few people I know, but I'm guessing none of them saw me or would remember if they did." He smiled: "I'm just like you. No alibi."

"I see."

After another brief, thoughtful pause, he said. "Between us, Sandy, in my opinion, Abel Mortenson was a one-man pestilence. There've been occasions, over the years, when I'd have liked nothing more than to eradicate him. There have definitely been times when I was probably a great deal more 'motivated' than I was on this occasion. I managed to restrain myself then. And I did so now. So, no, I didn't kill him." He paused and raised his eyebrows: "Did you?"

I had to laugh. If Martin Rose was feeding me bullshit, he was doing an artful job.

"No, Martin," I replied. "I did not." Both of us nodded in mutual commiseration.

Chapter Thirteen

Friday, March 5, 5:30 p.m.

A Brief Recess

I t was after five when I left Martin Rose and headed back across Campus toward my office. Capitol Way was heavy with State employees heading home for the weekend. The parking lots were emptying out. And I realized how little I was looking forward to my Friday evening Seattle commute and the long, lonely weekend ahead.

In few minutes, I'd be walking right past Paula McPhee's office.

I gave it some thought. I could call or text her, of course. Russ Kutscher, my friend and the Governor's Policy Advisor on Natural Resources had an office just down the hall from Paula's. Maybe I could simply stop off and see if Russ was still in. It would be a great excuse to just look in Paula's door and see if she was free for dinner.

Yes, I knew how circuitous that was. And, okay, so maybe I didn't really need such a cautious approach. But I was still very unsure where I stood with Paula. I didn't want to screw this up.

The Governor's policy shop may have been a prestigious place to work, but it was actually located in the dim, musty basement of the old Insurance Building. Russ was there but in a hurry to leave on a Friday evening, so we only had time for a brief conversation. I got a decisive "probably not" when I asked whether the Governor might be willing to veto the sport priority bill if it passed. I needed to keep that thing bottled up in Committee. As Russ and I walked together down the hall towards the office entrance, I could see Paula's door was open and her light was on.

I was in luck. I said good-bye to Russ and headed toward Paula's office.

She and I had been friends for years, ever since she was just starting out as a legal staffer for Aaron Nicolaides some years back when Aaron was House Speaker. It was only very recently, however, that we'd begun to develop a closer relationship.

She'd come a long way in the past three years. Business and Commerce was a plum position on the Governor's policy staff. And she'd made a strong go if it. She was smart, savvy, a hard-worker, and could be trusted. She knew the business world. And, at this point, she knew the legislative landscape as well as anyone.

Paula had been a couple of years behind me in law school at the UW. I had no clear impression of her from that time other than as studious, intense, and seemingly oblivious to the stir she inevitably caused among her male fellow law-students as she walked down the halls in the Condon Building on her way to her next class. Now she was a single mom with a child adopted during a former marriage. But she was still one of the smartest people on the Governor's staff—a wiz at business and respected by everyone I knew who'd met her. She was definitely making her mark.

From the day we'd run into one another again after I started lobbying, I'd found Paula appealing. She was quite attractive, with short, stylish, black hair and piercing dark eyes. What drew me, however, was her thoughtful quality. At times, in unguarded moments, she'd look pensive, almost sad, as if she carried a heavy burden. But then she'd suddenly surprise me with some startling insight or with a smile so engaging it would send a chill down my spine. Even so, it had taken me several years before I'd asked her out. I was put off, perhaps, by her intensity. Once she was focused on something, nothing could divert her; it was all about her work. Would she actually be interested in something so frivolous as a nice dinner, a show, or some kind of outing? I was never sure.

Over the past few months, however, we'd been out together maybe half a dozen times and, for the first time since my wife died, I found myself considering a new relationship. On a couple of those occasions, like the previous Sunday afternoon, Marissa had joined us in a daytime outing. I liked that; it gave Paula and me a chance to get to know each other in a more informal way. She was also a great mother—very protective of Marissa. It was a quality I appreciated. She was obviously doing an excellent job at raising her daughter—Marissa was a great kid. Today, Paula looked particularly at ease. Pleased with herself, even. Maybe things were going well for someone, at least, if not for me. She was, as usual, perfectly put together in a stylish professional pant-suit, a cream-colored silk blouse, and an interesting pin that looked to be made of petrified wood.

I pushed her door back a little and, when she looked up, I said, "Interested in dinner?"

She glanced at the clock on her desk, then at the open file. She is great with people, but I believe at heart, Paula is essentially an introvert. It wasn't in her DNA not to calculate almost everything. I was thinking this was going to be a "no way." But then I got that incredible grin: "Sure, why not," she said. "Let me call my neighbor to see if she can look after Marissa. Then I'll be right with you."

Even in early March, the days were definitely getting longer. It was still light and the gentle northerly breeze no longer stung with winter's chill as Paula and I made the brief walk together down Capitol Way. We found a back table at the Lemon Grass Restaurant in downtown Olympia. As we sat, I couldn't help looking across at her and thinking how strikingly attractive she was. You wouldn't have expected it from her name, but Paula was partly Native American with a distant family connection to the Swinomish Tribe. She was too far removed to be a Tribal member—too far to have even mentioned it in her law school application. But it was there in her features if you looked for it. Who knows, maybe in some way it was also there in her intense, goal-focused personality.

She'd grown up in rural Skagit County. Her dad grew potatoes on a family farm that had been first settled by Paula's great grandfather, a Scottish immigrant. He'd met and married a young Swinomish woman. They'd diked back the waters of the Skagit River and Skagit Bay and tilled the fertile land behind. The family had been there ever since.

But Paula wanted more than a life on the farm.

Paying for college and law school had, I gathered, been a real struggle for her. With help from her family and a succession of part-time jobs, she'd pulled it off. She didn't talk much about her brief marriage after law school, but her husband had apparently turned out to be something of a vagabond. Paula was totally devoted to her adopted daughter, Marissa, who was now about twelve. Marissa was a

Northwest Indian, also Swinomish as I understood it. As far as I knew, the ex-husband had been out of the picture for years.

Paula's job was one I knew she deserved. Before law school, she'd already earned an MBA. Her Master's thesis had actually been published in a scholarly journal. It was all about how a socially-responsible, regulated capitalist economy was essential to prosperity. Unlike me, she had a very specific, long-term career goal: she wanted a business practice with a large, successful law firm. If she could first make her mark in the public policy arena, she might be able to bypass the usual big-firm associate scramble for billable hours, clients, and status. Instead, she hoped to come in directly as a partner with a settled reputation and a ready clientele.

That was why, some years back after completing law school, she'd gone to work as a legal staffer for the House Democratic Leadership led by then House Speaker, Aaron Nicolaides. Nicolaides, also a lawyer and now out of office, was, what else, now a lobbyist—a Government Relations Specialist with the law firm of Morganthau, Staley, and Rimes. The firm's current Senior Partner, the son of its original founder, was Nelson Morganthau, a life-long Democrat and a heavy-hitting supporter and contributor to Paula's boss, Governor Carl Brown. As might have been anticipated, Governor Browne was a big supporter of Morgenthau's clients. Recently, Paula had ended up again working closely with Nicolaides.

Paula and I were one the same page on most political issues. Whenever we were together, we tended to fall naturally into conversation about partisan politics. "Your fishermen going to vote Republican in the Governor's race next year?" she asked me after the waitress had brought our coffee.

"Probably," I said. "They're essentially small business people. Don't trust government. Want to be left alone."

She arched one eyebrow and nodded ironically. "They do look for help, though, when they need it to catch their share of the public salmon resource."

I laughed. "Yes, that they do. If they didn't, I'd be defending DUIs in Seattle Municipal Court instead of here in the State Capitol sharing a nice dinner with a beautiful woman."

I was graced with a brief smile, but she was headed somewhere. "What would it take to get them to vote for a Democrat?"

"It probably wouldn't be easy. But I can tell you what would help."
I'd actually given this a lot of thought.

"Okay."

"As you say, the wild, open-water fisheries in our state are a shared, public resource. But they are managed as if they were some kind of private preserve. The right to catch fish is loosely allocated among competing user groups based mostly upon their history or 'prior claim,' their political clout, and the current biases in vogue at the Department of Fish and Wildlife." I paused, aware that I tended to launch forth on this topic. "You sure you want to know? I can become a terrible bore on this, if you let me."

"Consider me warned."

"Well, given that, it's no surprise that the various user groups fight over who gets to catch what. With no standards for what is right and fair, and with the decisions made in the political arena, of course they fight. It all plays out in ugly confrontations before the Legislature."

"So, what would you do about it?"

"I'd make some rules. Suppose, the Governor's Office directed the Department to establish basic principles for fishery resource allocation. First priority would be resource protection. But there'd also be criteria like maximizing economic worth, respect for valued cultures and social institutions, protecting fish-dependent communities, basic fairness, and, yes, history and prior claim. Stuff like that.

"We'd have a public process that, based on those principles, made the rules for how harvest was allocated among interested groups—excepting the Tribes, of course. It would all be in writing. With a clear rationale. We'd all be arguing off the same page in the same place over the same thing. Instead of an annual legislative free-for-all over who gets priority, we'd have some structure, legitimized expectations. And there'd be some sense that the outcome was reasoned and had a semblance of fairness. If we did that, it would be the last time you ever saw BS legislation like the current sport priority bill or like this deceptive, mean-spirited initiative we've got coming up on the ballot in November."

She laughed, it wasn't often that I'd seen Paula actually laugh. Obviously, she was getting more of an answer than she'd expected.

"Oh, and one other thing," I added. "You'd also see both sport and commercial fishermen openly supporting protections for salmon habitat."

"Wow," she said. "You *have* given this some thought."

"Sorry about that."

"If the Governor did all that, you think the commercial fishermen would vote for him, even though he's a horrible Democrat?"

"I think they'd vote for Lucifer if he promised a settled, dependable system of harvest allocation that was removed from politics and grounded in fairness. I might be out of a job, but I'd have happy clients."

"Have you ever discussed this with Russ?"

That made me smile. "Russ Kutcher thinks I'm a naïve idealist. 'Never going to happen,' is his answer."

At this point, our spring rolls arrived and we both settled in to eat.

"This is good," she said between bites. "More civilized that my usual fare of late."

"Plastic-wrapped sandwiches?"

"More like 'Norma Burgers' on the fly." She was referring to a widely-admired local hamburger place about ten miles north of Olympia, just off the I-5 exit at Nisqually. Norma's Burgers was a common stopover on the drive to Seattle, well-known by most Olympians and especially by Seattle to Olympia commuters. For a small woman, Paula did appreciate a hamburger.

"So, what about you? I assume you have your hands full with Fortuna." Paula was managing the Governor's legislative effort to get through the economic development package for the Bellevue-based high-tech powerhouse.

"Understatement," she said succinctly.

Last fall, Fortuna, a global leader in high tech, had proposed a massive investment in a new local computer center to service the growing market in cloud computing. With its cheap, reliable energy, skilled high-tech work force, and relaxed but business-friendly lifestyle, the Northwest was perfect for their venture. Fortuna had tentative partnerships with Microsoft, Amazon, and several other local high-tech companies. It hoped to create a hardware hegemony in the exploding global market for cloud services.

But for all that to pencil out, Fortuna needed help. They needed improvements to a State highway that would provide access to their new facility. They needed an expedited path through local development permitting. They needed a preferred rate under the State's Business and Occupation tax. And they needed a sales tax exemption on their purchases of construction related services and materials and on computer equipment. It would all add up to a lot of money.

All that help was, hopefully, to be delivered in the form of what those of us working the hill had come to call the "Fortuna Package," a group of bills now making their way through the Legislature. It turned out that Fortuna was one of the Morganthau Firm's, and hence one of Aaron Nicolaides' best clients. That, along with Paula's former relationship with Nicolaides and her current job as Business and Commerce policy staff, made it only natural that Governor Browne would assign her the responsibility for helping Nicolaides shepherd the Fortuna package through.

"How are you feeling about your chances?" I asked her.

"A lot better now that the 'Ds' are back in charge," she said. "They've done this kind to thing before. Twice for Boeing. Why not Fortuna? New jobs. Stronger tax base. Everyone wins."

"Yeah," I said. "But some maybe more than others."

"None of the people with a good job, out buying a new home or a car, will be complaining," she said.

I had to agree. Until that moment, it had not occurred to me that Fortuna, and those involved with its investment incentives package, might have had motive to remove Abel Mortenson. The post-Mortenson switch to Democratic control of the Senate affected almost everything—including the Fortuna package. Obviously, a lot of money was involved, as well as some very powerful people. Even Paula, for that matter.

It was still hard to see Senator Mortenson's murder as some calculated assassination by powerful interests performed by a highly-organized professional killer. The knife seemed more like a weapon of opportunity. A stabbing also seemed more personal and risky than some cold business proposition. It didn't add up.

I realized my mind had wandered. "Where's this facility going to be?" I asked. "Have they decided?"

"They have an option on the land. Up in the Snoqualmie Valley, not far from Carnation. It's actually one of the issues. Site's right in the middle of farm country. Thing's going to employ a bunch of people and generate new development pressure on the whole area. Much of it is currently in agriculture. King County's concerned and the local farmers are up in arms. Residential development out there runs counter to King County's Master Plan. Fortuna's asking for help on it."

"What can you do about that?" I asked.

"Well, a couple of those farms up there are applicants on this year's WWRP farm easement list. Fairly well down the list. Owners are well-respected farmers in the area. Might help settle down the opposition if we could bump up the WWRP appropriation." She rolled her eyes. "On top of everything else."

I had to smile at that. "Everything costs money."

"Yep. And more trips to Seattle. Don't know how you do that commute."

With our "from time-to-time" relationship, I didn't always know exactly what Paula was up to. I was aware that her work with Aaron Nicolaides on this Fortuna deal involved a lot of meetings in Seattle. She'd been making that trip almost as often as I did.

"Oh, well," I said. "There's always Norma's Burgers."

With that, something new crossed her face. "There is that," she said, but the light banter was gone. She had become serious again.

"How's Marissa?" I asked. Last Sunday she'd mentioned that her daughter had been facing some kind of bullying at school.

"Hard to tell," she said, her tone darkening. "She won't talk about it. I was in there, yesterday. Met with the Vice Principal. Not all that smart. Guess they're trying."

My guess was that some hapless Vice Principal had been set decisively back on target by Paula McPhee. She was protective of her daughter. It was something else I admired.

She pulled her phone out and glanced at it, checking the time. Then she folded her napkin and placed it on the corner of the table. "Marissa," she said by way of explanation. There were probably limits on how long she could ask her neighbor to look after her daughter.

Moments later we'd paid our bill and were out on the sidewalk headed back up toward the Capitol. "Were you around for the big event on Monday?" I asked her. We'd spent Sunday afternoon and evening together. I hadn't seen her since.

We both knew what I was talking about. "Nope. On the road. Meeting at two-thirty in Bellevue."

"Not a lot of disappointment around here, over his passing."

"Not that I've seen."

It was about eight by the time we'd walked up from town, cut across the Capitol Campus back past the Winged Victory Statute and Paula's office in the Insurance Building, and were standing on the sidewalk on Water Street just outside my office. This was where we parted company. "I need to get back to Marissa," she told me. "Thanks for dinner; it was nice." She turned to walk away. Then she stopped as if she'd remembered something. She turned back, dug down deep into her purse, and looked puzzled for a moment. Then, with a chagrinned shake of the head, she closed her purse again, smiled, shrugged, turned, and without a look back, headed off up the sidewalk in the direction of her home and her daughter.

Our parting had seemed abrupt. As I headed inside, I found myself feeling somehow abandoned. I had no right to feel like that. I hadn't expected anything out of this evening. Paula had somehow reminded me that, whenever I made a move to get close, she seemed to withdraw. For the umpteenth time, I was also reminded that she was a person on a mission. A driven personality.

I wasn't sure she really wanted me around or, for that matter, if I truly wanted to be along for the ride.

Chapter Fourteen

Saturday, March 6, 1:00 p.m.

Old Business

Senator Abel Mortenson's memorial service was held at an impressive Presbyterian Church in Bellingham on the Saturday following his death. Presumably, everyone present had known the man and, like me, came anyway. The entire event proved our astonishing capacity to suffer irony in silence.

County Assessor Phil Sheridan, the man with the inside track at winning Mortenson's place in the Senate, gave a heartfelt eulogy. Politicians of both parties were present though, on balance, the Republicans looked more broken up about Mortenson's passing than did his Democratic colleagues. Very few of the commercial fishermen I represented made it to the service. They probably owed the dead Senator a great deal more than most of those who were there. I understood the fishermen's feelings. In life, the Senator had been important to them. In death, not so much.

Mortenson's wife Mary was the only person present who looked truly broken up over his passing. Whatever the rest of us might have thought of the man as a Senator, his home life looked to have been a very different story. His widow's genuine grief contrasted starkly with the indifferent faces on most of the rest of the crowd. I suppose, in any murder, one should look first to those who were closest to the deceased, but it was my impression that Mary Mortenson was the last person to have wanted her husband dead.

I had initially planned to leave after the service but I changed my mind at the last minute and joined the long line of headlit vehicles driving together to the cemetery. That's when I realized Mortenson was about to be laid to rest at the same place where my wife was buried. When the services finally ended and people began to disperse, I wandered off among the stones in search of Susan's grave.

She had a small plot at the far edge of the property beneath an overhanging tree.

Susan had been in her twenties when she'd died. She was the daughter of a Bellingham fisherman and, just like me, she'd worked her way through college fishing for salmon on her father's boat. At the time, she was the only fisherman's daughter I knew of working in the fleet as a boat-puller like me. When I was a kid, we'd see their boat from time to time on the grounds in Alaska. I knew who she was, but it wasn't until much later, after I was through law school and out of the Navy that we actually met. That happened at, of all places, the Whatcom County Courthouse where she was working in the Superior Court Clerk's office and I was filing papers as a young attorney. We hit it off immediately and the small matter of a ninety-mile drive between my home in Seattle and hers in Bellingham did nothing whatsoever to dampen our relationship.

We were married a few months later. It was bit over a year after that she was buried here, the casualty of a dark night and a drunk driver.

I stood under that tree in the cold Bellingham mist for nearly an hour before, finally, I returned to my car and made a long, depressing slog back to Seattle in a pouring rain.

Chapter Fifteen

Wednesday, March 10, 9:45 a.m.

Public Discourse

W hen I saw the TV evening news on the Monday of the week following the Senator's death, I knew we were in for it. The coverage could not have been more cleverly designed to gin up public outrage.

How could such a thing happen right on grounds of our own State Capitol?

Who could do something like this; was it a terrorist?

Why hadn't the authorities identified the killer and made an arrest?

What impact would this have on the orderly conduct of government?

Commentators had picked it up and were adding fuel. But the origins were clear to anyone inclined to look. There were always one or two highly vocal elected officials who loved to pose as brave guardians of liberty standing up in the face of personal risk.

By Tuesday, the actual absence of any such existential threat had apparently become irrelevant. Its absence did not prevent the Senate, that morning, from adopting a floor resolution for a "thorough and complete investigation" into the death of Senator Abel Mortenson and for recommended "changes in law or appropriation which might be needed to assure the safety of our public officials" or which might be required to "create a secure climate within which elected representatives might, effectively and without intimidation, conduct the people's business." Tuesday morning, I'd spent an hour or so in the Senate Gallery watching the proceedings while on my phone calling fishermen asking them to attend and testify at the sport priority hearing the following day.

The resolution had been referred to the Senate Committee on Law and Justice and placed in the capable hands of its new Democratic Chair, Senator Arlo Devine of the 37th Legislative District in Central Seattle. Rising to the moment, Senator Devine had immediately scheduled hearings for the following day, Wednesday, one week and two days after Senator Mortenson's death. The hearing had been scheduled for ten a.m., a time calculated to make it convenient for Seattle reporters to drive down to Olympia, secure their quotes and pixels, and then file their reports well in advance of the evening news.

This previously unscheduled hearing would bump several other pending bills, potentially causing them to lose their positions for hearing and, therefore, for any chance of passage. Any of those bills might have been argued to be considerably more in the public's interest than a largely worthless inquiry disrupting an, as yet incomplete, police investigation.

This was the death of a fellow Senator. This was a matter of public safety. This threatened the very workings of our democracy.

It also promised to be pure theatre. Even if nothing whatever came of it, the whole show would, at least, be informative for those of us who kept our fingers on the pulse of the Legislature.

So, of course, I needed to be there.

I wasn't alone. When I entered the Cherberg Building's first floor hallway at about quarter to ten on Wednesday, the place was already packed. I worked my way through the crowd and camera lights and went directly into the hearing room, the largest one available, and was lucky to find a seat. There wasn't a lobbyist I knew who wasn't there. Many of them, like me, were ignoring the "turn off phones" signs, but all of us had our ringtones muted—nobody was going to anger a committee of legislators, no matter how important the call might be. A great many legislators not on the Committee were also present. There were a couple of agency directors as well, including David Prince from Fish and Wildlife. There were cameras everywhere. Reporters of every stripe were conducting interviews with people queuing up for the chance to have their thoughts immortalized.

I was just in time to see Senator Devine call the hearing to order and proceed immediately to the business of the day. A Committee staffer was called up to read the Senate Resolution that had launched the investigation and then to explain the legal foundations and authority of the Committee in this matter. There were several studious, nicely phrased questions from Members, all of whom were present and on time, perhaps for the first time in the Committee's recent history.

Finally, moving to the stars of the show, Senator Devine called up for testimony the head of the Washington State Patrol, Chief Lehan K. Orbison, Jr. and the officer who was leading the Patrol's investigation, Lieutenant Nathan Wilson, head of the Patrol's General Investigations Unit.

Chief Orbison looked right at home in this setting of intense scrutiny. He made a few brief pithy remarks about the Patrol's scrupulous enforcement of the law and its commitment to professionalism. Then he turned it over to his capable subordinate, Lieutenant Wilson.

Unlike his Chief, Wilson looked very much like this was the last place he wanted to be. He did, however, do a dry but competent job of summarizing what had been learned from forensic evidence gathered at the scene, and what they currently believed about the nature of the crime. Wilson's matter-of-fact narrative went a long way toward letting some of the air out of the room and making the whole matter seem somewhat less momentous than might have at first appeared.

When the time came for questions, all that factuality and restraint evaporated. These Senators had a point to make. It wasn't every day you had the chance to act out before the cameras. Not one of the seven Committee Members opted to forgo that opportunity. Over the past week, I'd acquired some empathy for the Lieutenant. He had a difficult job to do. With this hearing, that job was going to get even more challenging. These fifteen minutes of fame were, for him, I imagined, fifteen minutes of hell.

If he'd been worried about being pinioned by incisive cross questioning, however, he needn't have been. It was the Committee Members who wanted to testify. In their view, any time spent by a witness in actually answering a question was time wasted. Each Member had a point to make, or several. The worst was Chairman Devine who constantly interrupted his colleagues to rephrase their questions more to his own liking. By the time one or the other of them wound down long enough for Wilson to reply, everyone had largely forgotten what he'd actually been asked. It didn't really matter what Wilson said, so long as it sounded reassuring.

Fortunately, reassuring was one of the Lieutenant's strengths.

By the time the Senate Law and Justice Committee had finally run out of collective breath, an hour and a half had passed and the Chair was announcing the hearing's adjournment to an almost empty room. Anything over about half an hour exceeded the press's attention span.

Who knew what would be reported in the evening news?

The one unsettling thing I learned was that Judith had been right about the time of death. The knife had nicked the spine and the coroner believed Mortenson might have been immobilized and lost consciousness quickly, but then have taken anything from a few minutes to nearly an hour to die. The Patrol was using my departure and Judith Bosch's return as the time frame within which the murder had been committed.

For me, the takeaways were that I wasn't entirely out of the woods and that the mystery of the Senator's murder was still a very long way from resolution. I'd also realized I'd acquired a few insights into the murder and I should probably go back to Lieutenant Wilson and renew my offer of help.

Chapter Sixteen

Wednesday, March 10, 11:00 a.m.

Temporary Accommodation Between Foes

One of the people I'd noticed in the hearing room earlier was none other than Clive Curtin, attending perhaps, like me, out of self-interest. He'd already left the hearing room before it occurred to me that this might be my best chance to catch up with him. He wasn't in the hallway. There was a small public space between the House and Senate office buildings, a paved circle with a bronze sundial in the center and surrounded by flower beds. People sometimes lingered there to talk when the weather was clear. Sure enough, there he was, wearing his usual dark, expensive-looking suit and tie, conversing with a small group of friends I assumed were his fellow anglers. They were probably struggling, as I was, to adapt to the legislative shake-up precipitated by Mortenson's death.

These were folks who would not be happy to see me. I headed in their direction anyway and managed to catch Curtin's eye and let him know with a wave that, when he had a chance, I'd like a word. I will say he didn't seem in any hurry to complete the conversation with his friends. I used the time to make a few calls. The group did break up soon after, and Curtin came over in my direction.

"Strange event," he said.

"Very," I agreed. "End of the day, it doesn't look to me like they know a damn thing."

"It sure doesn't."

"You probably know I was apparently the last person to see Mortenson alive."

"Well, hopefully not the *last*," he said, with a significant grin.

"Yeah, well, I was *not* the killer. I'm not sure, however, our Lieutenant Wilson is yet completely convinced of that. I assume Mortenson is why he was at your office the other day."

"Um hmm. So why were *you* there? You sure disappeared in a hurry. The Lieutenant make you nervous?"

I ignored his needling. "I noticed that you stopped by to see Senator Troy that morning. I guess while I was upstairs with Mortenson, you were down below talking to Troy."

He seemed surprised, maybe even chagrined that I'd known that. A little defensively, he said: "So where'd *you* go after *your* meeting?"

"Back to my office. Nobody saw me until Helen came back from lunch around one thirty. I was in the office working till Wilson and his boys showed up about three thirty that afternoon to ask me questions. It was the first I'd heard about the murder."

"Uh huh. So, no alibi?" He smiled when he said it; it wasn't the friendliest of smiles.

"No alibi," I said. Then, handed the opportunity: "How about you? Where were *you* when Mortenson was killed?"

At that he laughed, this time more good-naturedly. "I don't have an alibi either. I was headed back to Seattle. Stopped and paid cash for a burger and headed home."

"Norma's? At Nisqually?"

"How'd you know?"

"She makes a great burger."

"Yeah, well, I got caught in a hell of a traffic snarl trying to get back on the freeway. An accident at that intersection, just before you head up the on-ramp. I lost nearly an hour."

"It's a busy place, Clive. You see anyone that knows you?"

"Nah. No such luck." He gave it some further thought. "I did see someone I know, though. That woman that works in the Governor's office. McPhee, I think."

"Paula McPhee?"

"Yeah, that's her. She was just coming out of Norma's as I was going in. But she doesn't know me from Adam. Doesn't really do me any good." I remembered Paula had mentioned stopping for lunch that day, but she hadn't said it had been at Norma's.

Curtin looked at me thoughtfully. "You know, Dalton," he said. "There is something we should probably talk about. Has to do with the initiative. You got a few minutes?"

"Sure." We walked across the street to the Prichard Building to the small deli and coffee shop in the space that was once a reading room for the Washington State Library. It's right next to the Third House, the lobbyist's message center. It was still early for lunch so we easily found a table at a window facing back toward the sundial and with a nice view of the Capitol Building beyond. "So," I said once we had our coffees and were seated. "What's on your mind?"

Curtin looked uncomfortable, like he wasn't sure how to begin. Or, perhaps, if he should. "So, as you're aware," he said, apparently deciding to go ahead. "We've got our signature gatherers out on this initiative. They're doing pretty well. We feel we'll easily get the 250,000 or so we need to get it on the ballot. But, even so, maybe you've seen the news? Of late there've been some ugly conflicts between our gatherers and some of your fishermen."

I had read about that. Some of the commercial fisherman in the groups I represented were determined to slow down the signature effort. On their own, they'd decided to go in small groups to the park-n-rides, malls, big box stores, and other sites where they knew the anglers went to get signatures. When they found a signature-gatherer, they'd stand nearby and, whenever someone stopped to talk or read the petition, they'd approach them and argue the case for why the initiative was a bad idea and why the person shouldn't sign. This had the desired effect of driving people away—most people really don't want to get involved in some sort of public political argument while they're waiting for a bus or out shopping for groceries or a new toaster.

When the signature-gatherers tried to move elsewhere, the commercial guys followed, in effect stalking them. Sometimes even tailing them by car to an entirely new site. Some of these gatherers were volunteers. Some were "professionals" who were paid by the signature; not well-compensated work by any standard. None of them were prepared for this kind of public confrontation. There had been a number of yelling matches, and even a few fistfights, a couple of which had involved police or security personnel. One of them had resulted in assault charges.

"This hasn't yet blown up into a big deal in the press," Curtin continued. "If it continues, it will." He paused and looked me in the eye. "Is that something you want?"

It was a damn good question. A few more incidents like this, especially if one happened to be captured on someone's phone, and we could be facing a real problem. Signature-gatherers may, sometimes, be a nuisance, but people generally felt they were entitled to be there. The public wouldn't like it if they came to see commercial fishermen as a bunch of "bully-boys" who ganged up on citizen-volunteers trying to engage in normal civil discourse or who intimidated voters seeking to peacefully sign a public ballot initiative. With the right video, I could easily visualize a hell of a damaging story on TV news.

"No," I said. "No, it isn't."

I could understand why Curtin was concerned. I bet they were finding it hard enough to find volunteers to gather signatures without them needing to face this kind of thing. Every signature they couldn't gather with a volunteer would require a paid professional. This was probably costing them money. Even if their effort was well on track, it had to be a concern.

"The assault case in Snohomish County," he continued, "was filed as mutual charges—both parties were charged. The next one could easily go against your guys. It's them, after all, who are coming up and initiating these confrontations."

He was right. "I agree, Clive. It's got to stop. I'll talk with them about it." Even if these confrontations were slowing them down and costing them money, if the fights became a big story in the press, we'd end up with a black eye just when we needed to look like responsible citizens trying to earn an honest living.

From his look, I could tell Curtin was trying to judge how serious I was about following up; to decide whether he'd possibly made a mistake, maybe revealed a weakness, in mentioning it. "Thanks for mentioning this, Clive," I said, to set his mind at ease. "I appreciate it. I think we both have an interest in putting an end to this. We have a big meeting coming up on Friday. I'll bring it up and do what I can."

That seemed to satisfy him. He sat back, somewhat more relaxed, and took a sip of coffee. Then, looking at his watch, he sat up again and said: "I'm meeting someone for lunch. Probably better get going."

I nodded, took a last swallow myself, and we rose and headed for the door. I still wanted to hear Curtin's response to his Mortenson situation. Now, the brief relaxation of tension between us seemed to offer my best chance. As we left the building and walked together across the street and down in the direction of the Capitol Building, I took my shot.

"I gather Senator Mortenson was holding you up with that letter you wrote to all the sports fishing groups on the initiative. The one back in November."

That brought him to a full halt in the center of the busy sidewalk. "Who told you that?"

"Well," I said, "I guess, among others, you just did. As you know, it's hard to keep a secret in this place." I held up my hands. "Don't' worry about it, Clive. You're far from alone. Anybody who ever dealt with that SOB had problems with him. Me included. Even if I hadn't heard it from a good source, it wouldn't have been hard to guess. What did he want?"

Curtin took a deep breath and stood there a moment as he digested all this and took in the idea that his letter was no longer a secret. Then, he turned and we headed on down the sidewalk as he explained: "He wanted our support in the coming elections. Can you believe that? Wanted me to write a public endorsement in our Northwest Angler Magazine. After all the grief he's given us over the years. He's been in your pocket long as I can remember. There's no way I'd ever have trusted him to follow through. None of us would have."

"What did you tell him."

Curtin laughed. "Told him yes, of course. Then I just delayed things. Tried to keep him wondering, slow him down. With that letter in his hands, I knew it would come out sooner or later. Just figured the later the better."

I had to admit, it sounded plausible. Not far different from what I might have done.

As we parted company at the south entrance to the Capitol Building, we shook hands again. I didn't like the man any better than before, but our relationship had changed. It felt as if the past half-hour might have generated a thin margin of new mutual respect.

At one-thirty that same afternoon, Curtin's current sport priority bill came up for its re-scheduled hearing. Mortenson's successor as Chair, Senator Jimmy Fang, told me he'd hesitated to cancel the hearing since his predecessor had already committed to doing it. But Fang was, at least at that point, still disinclined to bring it up for a vote in executive session, and I already knew there was no executive session actually scheduled for the bill this week. Just to be sure, I'd done some further checking with other members of Natural Resources Committee and was feeling confident that the bill would never make it out, even if Fang changed his mind. The cutoff calendar would kill it if it wasn't voted out of Committee by early next week.

Meanwhile, the gillnet/seabird bill had finally moved out of Rules and was on the floor of the Senate. It might take a while to get a vote, but it had made it through to the last hurdle in record time. Based on Janice Burdell's vote count, the odds for its passage now looked good.

The one-thirty Natural Resources hearing was little more than a replay of similar events I'd worked over the past several years. My calls had paid off. I'd made sure the word also got out by email, text, and through a phone tree we still used for matters like this, so there was plenty of commercial fishing representation there. A bunch of my guys were all wearing bright neon-green baseball caps that said: "Save Commercial Fishing." This hearing was a serious matter for them. Fishing was how they earned their living. For many, it was a family business involving skills that had been handed down for generations or that they'd brought with them from the "old country." They were proud of what they did. Many of them had few alternatives. Even this trip to Olympia to testify would cost most of them the best part of their day, time they could ill afford.

Still, the event lacked some of the urgency we'd seen over these battles in years past. Witnesses who'd signed in on each side of the bill, pro or con, were called up to testify in little groups of three. It was the same, familiar players on each side with the usual arguments Each side claimed their fishery was most protective of the salmon resource. Each argued that they contributed more jobs and economic value. As usual, some of the non-professionals couldn't help rambling on and on before being gently but firmly cut off by the Chair at the end of their three minutes. Some were nervous and incoherent. There were stories, statistics, competing claims, pain, and bravado.

But, on the whole, it felt like I was observing a sport fishing community that had finally lost any real hope that they would ever get anything done by these legislators. Their hopes were now pinned to their ballot initiative. Their testimony here came across as mostly pro-forma. Judging by the questions, or lack of them, from legislators, the Committee Members weren't much enthused either. It was all about to be decided by the voters; why should a legislator get in the middle of it? When the Committee finished with our bill and I got up to leave, I was feeling more confident than ever that this bill was dead.

Apparently, Clive Curtin agreed. I ended up walking out the hearing room door just behind him. In the crowded hall, as we about to go separate ways, he turned back and gave me a disdainful grin and a shake of the head.

"Waste of a perfectly good afternoon," was all he said.

As he headed away down the hall, I considered again whether he could possibly have murdered a Washington State Senator. I had to admit I'd been impressed with what he'd said this morning about his stop at Norma's Burgers at Nisqually. Of course, he had no one who could testify that he was there. At least as far as I was concerned, his account had seemed much too specific to be manufactured. I would, of course, ask Paula about it. If she had actually been there as he'd said, while it wasn't definitive, it was certainly a point in his favor.

While Clive Curtin was not to be underestimated as an enemy, I had my doubts about him as the killer. I still believed the culprit would turn out to be one someone who'd been pushed beyond breaking by the Senator's hateful intrigues; there were a good many people who might qualify. Finding the guilty party, however, was proving to be elusive.

Chapter Seventeen

An Off-Calendar Encounter

The Cherberg Building hallway was packed with people. Some, like me, were leaving hearings that were ending; others were waiting to enter the ones scheduled to begin at three-thirty. So, as I turned in the crowd to make for the back exit in the direction of my office, I literally bumped into someone. As I apologized, I realized it was Al Borichevsky, the State Patrol Lieutenant I'd worked with briefly some years before and who I'd been meaning to call.

Back when I was still practicing law, and lobbying was still just a small part of my work, I'd had a client who'd been cited for a fisheries violation. I'd stopped by the State Patrol Headquarters to try for a disinterested yet professional perspective on how the Fisheries Patrol officer had handled that arrest. They'd handed me off to Borichevsky.

Borichevsky was the Patrol's Media Relations and Government Liaison officer whose job apparently included fielding miscellaneous public inquiries like mine. Within the limits you'd expect, he'd been very helpful. My understanding was that he was a fully trained, qualified, and experienced police officer. I suspected, however, that his urbane style had redirected his career into an area of specialization many of his colleagues might find abhorrent. He seemed comfortable in his work. Like most other members of the Patrol I'd come in contact with, he wore the uniform on a daily basis, and he seemed comfortable with that as well.

Since that day, Al had been a familiar face around the Capitol, someone with whom I'd occasionally shared a nod and a wave of greeting. Like many of the agency liaison people, he didn't hang out with ordinary lobbyists over at the "Third House" message center in the Prichard Building, the "Gulch" as we called it. We had very different beats and hadn't had another occasion to deal with each other.

Seeing him there, however, reminded me that I still had some questions about the State Patrol's role in the Mortenson investigation and that he might also be a source of information about his colleague, Lieutenant Nathan Wilson. I'd been conscious that I should go over to the Admin Building and talk with Wilson again but had been putting it off. Al might be my best chance to glean a little insight into just who Wilson was and how he saw the world.

"Hey, Lieutenant," I said, shaking his hand after apologizing for running into him. "You headed in for a hearing?"

"Just got out," he said. He shook his head and frowned: "Budget."

"Great fun."

"Oh yeah."

"Look," I said. "Any chance I could buy you a cup of coffee?" In response to his puzzled look, I added: "There's a matter I'm dealing with that involves the Patrol. Maybe you could help me clear up a couple of questions."

He hesitated, but only briefly. Then, "Sure, why not. Make it a hot chocolate, and I'm in."

The Capitol Building basement had a small, self-serve coffee bar joined up with four or five small windowless rooms that had been married together in a "creative" remodel some years before. Tables were tucked here and there in the various nooks and corners, making it possible to relax there and even sometimes have a private conversation. This late in the day the place was nearly empty.

"So, what can I do for you?" he asked as we sat.

"Well, I have a couple of questions about the State Patrol. I gather you guys have jurisdiction over crimes on the Capitol Campus?"

He took a sip of his cocoa and took his time answering. "This about Senator Mortenson? He was Natural Resources, right? So, I guess you two saw a lot of each other?"

"Yeah, it is," I said. "He was an important ally." Al gave me a doubtful look that made me add: "Yes, and a pain in the butt, sometimes."

"Sounds like about what I've heard. Why do you ask?"

"As it happens, I'm, I guess you'd say, connected to the case.

I was Mortenson's last appointment before he died. His death has a lot of ramifications for my clients. I think I was probably one of the first people your colleague, Lieutenant Wilson, interviewed after the murder."

"I see." He still looked puzzled. "And you want to know about our investigative jurisdiction because…?"

"Um, look. What I really want to know is, how common it is for the Patrol to head up a murder investigation?"

He laughed. "No. What you *really* want to know is whether we know what the hell we're doing, right?"

I smiled. "Yeah, that too. I was at that hearing this morning, and…"

"And you weren't impressed?"

"I guess I'd just say, it doesn't seem like much is happening on the case."

"I was there, up front with the troops." I hadn't seen him; I'd probably been looking at the back of his head. "Look, um, it's Sandy, right?"

"Sandy, yeah."

"Look, Sandy, keep in mind it has only been a bit over a week since the murder, not that long. I can tell you this. There isn't anyone better qualified to lead that investigation than Nate Wilson. No one."

"I have to admit, Lieutenant…"

"Al." He smiled.

"Al. I have to admit that Wilson seems a little out of his depth. I feel like I know a few things that could help, at least about the political dimension. I'm tempted to stop in for a visit. I'm uncomfortable, however, just barging in on him and, basically, implying that he doesn't know what he's doing. I'm also, most likely, on his list of possible suspects. So, it all seems a bit pushy. And I'm concerned he could take it wrong."

"Ah. I see." Borichevsky took another thoughtful sip of his hot chocolate. "Let me tell you a story," he said. "Maybe set your mind at ease."

"Okay."

"Let me just start by telling you that Nate Wilson is one of the most qualified, capable officers I know in the Washington State Patrol. He's got a degree in Criminal Justice from the University of Washington Tacoma. He spent time on street patrol and later was a Detective with the Tacoma Police Department, a good part of that in homicide. He's been with the State Patrol for something like twenty years now. If there was any justice in the world, he'd be running the place. Instead, Lieutenant is probably as high as he's ever going to go."

He had my attention. I'd known none of this.

"A few years back," Borichevsky continued. "Wilson was helping local authorities with a highly-publicized hit-and-run on Interstate 90, east of Seattle. Four people died, including a widely-respected member of the Bellevue City Council. The chain-reaction accident had been started with a side-swipe by a hit-and-run passenger car. Based on the reported behavior of the car as it fled the scene, the driver had probably been intoxicated. No one had caught the license number. There was no description of the driver, and not much about the car. All they had was a small paint sample. With that, they'd come up with a color, a likely make, and an approximate year. Other than that, they were nowhere.

"The press had been all over them. Tensions were high. Fortunately, as it turned out, what little they knew had found its way into the media.

"Finally, after three very long weeks, they caught a break. The parents of an eight-year-old boy had called local police to report that their son thought he'd seen scratches on a neighbor's car. It was the right make and maybe the right color. Unfortunately, the car was kept in a closed, attached garage. The parents said it was still in use and said their neighbor often came home late and inebriated.

"It was pretty shaky for a warrant.

"Wilson proposed staking out the house until the car was driven somewhere, follow it, and then with the car parked in some public place, take a close look, photograph the damage, and, if there was enough to go on, either seize the car under exigent circumstances or then go get the necessary warrant.

"But Wilson's boss, our current Chief, overruled him.

"Instead, they ginned up some paperwork and convinced a friendly judge to issue the warrant. Two detectives were sent to the man's home. He refused to talk and, of course, demanded a lawyer. The detectives examined the car, found the damage, and seized it. Paint trace analysis later conclusively linked the car to the accident.

"Wilson disagreed with Orbison about the approach, and everyone in the office knew it. Two months later, the warrant and resulting evidence, the car, the paint trace analysis, it was all thrown out by the

Trial judge. The offender walked free and Orbison, who since became our Chief, was badly embarrassed—at least among his colleagues in the Patrol.

"Nobody needed further proof of Wilson's competency. I'm sure you know exactly how this works, right? From that point forward, the drill on Nate Wilson has been that he isn't a 'team player.' He was right, but he's been taking the heat for it ever since.

"You know, Wilson has detectives that work for him. He could have assigned this out. You should be happy he took it on himself. He may not be some big city homicide detective, but I've got to tell you, Sandy. If I were in your position, I can't think of anyone I'd rather have on it."

That was an impressive testimonial. I didn't know what to say in response. Especially since It wasn't lost on me that Al Borichevsky's own story also tended to confirm my impression. Clearly Wilson was an experienced and capable detective who knew his stuff. To me, however, it seemed clearer than ever that he was also a man who tended to ignore the political dimension of things—what my job was all about.

Given Al's job, he was my best chance to learn the answer to my next question: "So, given what you've just told me," I said. "Do you think Lieutenant Wilson is politically savvy enough to sort through the interests and relationships at work in this place, the stuff that might have provided motive for the murder of a State Senator in the middle of a legislative session?"

My question did bring Al up short. He paused in thought.

"I'm asking," I continued, "because, as I said, I'd like to offer him some help. But, given my position, if I do that, I'm not sure how it's likely to be received."

"Well, it probably depends on how serious he is about you as a candidate for perpetrator."

"That and how concerned he is about his own pride," I added.

"You know, he and I did talk about this case a few days back. He came to me to ask where, over here on the hill, he might go for some answers. I suggested he talk with the legislative liaison people, my counterparts, for the agencies whose issues came through Senator Mortenson's Committee. That'd be Fish and Wildlife, Natural Resources, and the like. I think he went off and did exactly what I'd suggested. I've got to say, he didn't seem particularly slow about asking for *my* advice. He just seemed to appreciate it. Honestly, I think you should just go for it. I don't think you've got much to worry about, on that front."

With that, Borichevsky checked the time on his phone and announced he had to get back to the office. I thanked him as profusely as I could before he left. He'd been a big help.

As I sat there alone, finishing my coffee deep in the basement of the Capitol Building, I realized with a sinking feeling that I was out of excuses.

I would have to go in for that talk with Lieutenant Nathan Wilson and hope for the best.

Chapter Eighteen

Wednesday, March 10, 4:20 p.m.

An Uneasy Collaboration

As I entered the General Administration Building late that Wednesday afternoon and headed toward the State Patrol Headquarters office, I felt like I was about to poke a large bear with a very short stick. Both Wilson and I needed to get this matter resolved, however. For my own peace of mind, I wanted to talk with someone in authority about what I'd learned and suspected.

When Wilson walked into the reception area where I stood waiting, he looked surprised to see me. "Dalton," he said. "What can I do for you?"

"Got a few minutes, Lieutenant?"

"Sure, come on in. My office is right down here."

His office was not luxurious but it also wasn't the cubbyhole I'd somehow imagined. He headed up a statewide unit within the Patrol and I didn't think they had all that many Lieutenants. He sat behind his desk and motioned me to an upholstered guest chair just in front of it. So far so good, I told myself.

"Lieutenant, I don't want to be acting out of turn or in any way compromising your work on the Mortenson case. I hope you understand that." He looked a bit puzzled, so I quickly continued. "But you probably already know that I've talked with some of the people who may be involved in this." I could tell by his humorless look that he definitely did. "I hope you appreciate that these are people I work with all the time."

"I take it you're not good about taking instruction?"

Not the best start, but at least he didn't sound truly angry. "You know, Lieutenant, Senator Mortenson's murder isn't a topic I'm likely to avoid in most conversations on the hill these days," I said, as deferentially as I could. Then, considering his look, I decided I'd better add: "But, yeah, I've asked a few questions. The Senator's death has an impact on the clients who are paying me to look out for their interests. It isn't just idle curiosity. Or meddling. And I'm here, today, because, after the hearing this morning, I'm wondering: Could I possibly be useful?"

With a little resigned shake of the head, he finally spread his hands open on his desk, stared at me intently for a moment. With the briefest of smiles: "Well, all right," he said. "So, now you're here. Why don't you go ahead and tell me what you've been up to? And what you think you know?"

It was better than a flat "no." I was starting to wonder if I'd misjudged him. "Ever since you came by my office last week," I said. "I've been worrying about this thing."

"Okay."

"You did a great job at the hearing today, but I still can't help feeling that it has to be an uphill battle for an outsider to feel their way through the, well… the complications of this place." I was struggling for the right approach. To me, this seemed like a guy who hated politics. Someone who changed channels when the news came on. I just wasn't sure how he'd take what I was saying. "I don't know if I've learned anything you don't already know, but I'd like to share a few things with you. If I can do so without seeming, um… arrogant, I guess. I'd like to offer whatever help I can."

"I see."

"At the same time, I expect I'm maybe a suspect, so perhaps none of that makes sense, but, there it is. That's why I'm here."

Wilson smiled. He was also shaking his head, but it all looked genuine. "Well, why don't we start with you filling me in on what you think you've learned? Maybe we can go from there." It felt positive. He didn't act offended. I hoped he didn't think I'd essentially told him he couldn't be relied on to know what he was doing. He also hadn't actually refused my help or refused to fill me in. He was a proud man. This could be the only way he'd accept my help. If he was willing to discuss this, maybe it meant I was no longer near the top of his suspect list.

For the next twenty minutes or so, I told him what I'd learned. I was pleased and, I'll admit, surprised as it became clear that he had, in one way or another, managed to find his own way to everyone I'd spoken with about Mortenson. After each of those conversations, I'd written down some notes to help later refresh my memory. I referred to those notes now. He made only a very few interruptions or requests for more detail, but when he did, they seemed significant.

As I'd suspected, he was fully aware of the malfunctioning security camera. I was pleased to learn that Senator Troy had told him that Mortenson was alive and well in the back stairwell after I'd left for my office. Judith Bosch had, apparently, told him that, in that final meeting I'd had with the Senator it had been Mortenson, not me, who'd been yelling. Wilson had not been aware that Judith's father's dairy farm was up for a WWRP agricultural easement acquisition, that its inclusion in the WWRP budget was in question, nor of the importance of that to Judith and her family. He was also not aware of Martin Rose's stumble in testimony before House Natural Resources earlier this year and how it might have made Martin's job status uncertain. He didn't know that Senator Troy's wife had severe Alzheimer's, that Troy had missed some important appointments of late so he could be with her in Seattle, or that missing those appointments was very uncharacteristic for him.

We talked in some detail about Clive Curtin. As I'd learned from Judith Bosch, she'd told him about Curtin's letter and Mortenson's response to it. Wilson. He was apparently very concerned about Curtin's eleven-forty-five a.m. appointment just down the back stairs from Mortenson's office on the day of Mortenson's death. I told him about Curtin's claim that he stopped at Norma's Burgers on his way back to Seattle and that Curtin had mentioned being caught in a traffic jam from an accident at the Nisqually on-ramp. I said he'd also mentioned seeing Paula there who, according to Curtin, didn't know him.

He'd found most everyone involved, but I was surprised to realize that he didn't know about the "picture book," a directory of Washington State Lobbyists available on the Public Disclosure Commission website. "Just look at the firms and organizations they represent," I told him. "The ones that deal in natural resource issues like fisheries, mining, timber, and the like. Those will be the people that had to deal with Senator Mortenson."

He looked that up and seemed pleased to have the information. He also looked up and confirmed that there had, in fact, been a major accident at that I-5/Nisqually intersection at about twelve-twenty p.m. on that date. The accident was no secret; there had been a serious injury. It was still under active investigation. It had made the local papers, so Curtin could have learned about it and just used it as a prop, but I didn't think so. I planned to talk with Paula to see if she'd been there. Even if she didn't know or hadn't seen Curtin, the two items together did seem persuasive, at least to me.

Initially, I didn't mention my thought that the legislative effort to get incentives for Fortuna's big venture might have given someone involved a motive. It seemed awfully speculative, but then it came up indirectly. We were discussing the WWRP appropriation and Judith Bosch's father's dairy. I said: "You know, that appropriation might be important for other reasons. It's my understanding that some of the farmers up in the Snoqualmie Valley are very worried about the Fortuna Package."

He blew me away with his response to that one: "Fortuna Package?"

He hadn't heard of it. So, I filled him in. This was, apparently, all news to him.

"So, you're saying Mortenson's death might have an effect on the WWRP appropriation and thus help get this Fortuna deal through?"

"Yes, Lieutenant, but it's much more than that. There's a whole package of incentives involved: environmental impact rules, business and sales tax relief, expedited development permitting, a whole bunch of stuff. All of it is much more likely to pass now, with Mortenson gone."

His reaction made me realize that none of these broader ramifications had really sunk in even though I'd mentioned them in a general way when we'd first met last week at my office.

I continued: "But even that, even Fortuna, is just the tip of the iceberg," I said. "The impact is much bigger than just Fortuna. Mortenson's death could affect a great many of the bills currently moving through the Legislature, all kinds of things. With him out of the way, the Democrats are now taking over. When his replacement shows up, which will be soon, they'll be in the majority. But even now with them evenly split, at least on procedural matters the Lieutenant Governor, a Democrat, is the tiebreaker. Almost every bill before the Senate faces a dramatically altered landscape, including the State Budget."

He was stunned by that. "You're saying, all this could have been anticipated in advance?"

"By someone who was thinking about it, sure. It was all but a certain outcome."

He hadn't known about any of this. Moreover, from what I'd heard in the hearing that morning, they'd uncovered very little in the way of useful forensic evidence. The knife's handle had been wiped of prints and the rest of the office was so covered in them that they were essentially worthless. There were no identifiable hairs or fiber samples left in the Senator's splattered blood. No one had been caught running from the scene with bloody hands. With the vandalized security camera, there was no video record at the most likely point of entry. So here they were, looking desperately for a motive while the political fallout was so broad as to make almost anyone at the Capitol a suspect.

The Lieutenant's momentary dismay was understandable. The vast array of legislative prospects which had been dramatically and predictably transformed by Mortenson's death was overwhelming.

"Do you think this murder could have been something planned in advance?" I asked him when I'd finished filling him in.

"Well, if you mean technically 'premeditated,' sure, I think it could," he said. "Someone could easily have known the security camera would be down, that Mortenson would be in his office alone in a largely deserted building, and even that the knife was there." He didn't sound convinced.

"It would have been a very risky venture," I said.

"Yeah. That and a knife killing is awfully personal. It's harder to do than you might think—requires some strength. That or some serious anger. Someone who really hated this guy."

That was what I'd been thinking. "So not really a calculated killing?" I asked. "More likely to have been someone in a momentary rage?" That seemed awfully likely, given the Abel Mortenson I'd known.

"Maybe," he said, but he wasn't willing to speculate further about it.

At least I'd done the right thing and given him everything I knew. It was, after all, his job to find the killer. The only thing remotely concrete that I received from him in return was a photocopy of the painfully brief, inconclusive report from the Patrol's crime scene investigation which mentioned the added grisly detail that, before leaving the

Senator's office, the killer had, apparently, wiped their prints off the protruding handle of the knife with the Senator's own tie. The fact that Digger Troy had seen Mortenson alive after I left didn't let me off the hook (I could, of course, have returned a few minutes later), but it seemed to have eased Wilson's mind somewhat on my account. He'd been significantly more relaxed toward me than I remembered from our first encounter.

When I left Wilson's office that day, I felt incrementally relieved. From what I could see, and from what Al Borichevsky had told me, Wilson seemed to be an experienced detective and, for the first time, I felt the investigation was in capable hands. Before I walked out, of course he repeated his warning that I not be "tinkering around the edges" of his murder investigation. He reemphasized that he wouldn't hesitate to call me to account if he believed I was interfering. I could see his point, but the warning seemed less caustic, almost rote, as if he knew I'd probably disobey it. I believed he felt I'd added value and I was glad I'd gone by.

The Senator's murder was still in the radio news on Wednesday evening as I drove home. I wondered what my dad was making of all the press it had received since we'd talked last week. I waited till after sundown to call and caught him as he was just cleaning up after dinner.

"I take it you're not in jail," he said, only half joking.

"Not yet, Dad." I replied, in the same spirit. "I think, at this point, I'm mostly out of the woods. I spent an hour this afternoon with the State Patrol Lieutenant who's investigating the case. Helping him with a few things."

"Well," he said. "That sounds more like it. Seems like you could be of use if they'll let you."

That was my feeling as well. Based on my afternoon visit with Lieutenant Wilson, however, the prospect of finding the killer by identifying the motive now seemed all but hopeless. I felt further than ever from any real answers.

Chapter Nineteen

Thursday, March 11, 7:45 a.m.

An Independent Witness

I was fond of listening to audiobooks during my long, daily commutes down from Seattle. Thursday morning, I again tuned in to the local news instead. South of Tacoma, there was an Olympia station that provided excellent coverage of the Legislature. That's how I learned that Senator Digger Troy's wife, Joan, had died the night before.

I didn't know Troy well but I was saddened by the news. I'd only met his wife the one time on that local Conservation District bus tour visit to the Troy Ranch a few years back. She had, however, made an impression; she was so bright, charming, and alive. According to the reporter covering her death, Joan Troy had grown up and attended high school in Kirkland. She had family in the King County area and was to be buried in Bellevue. There was a local memorial service planned for Saturday in Kirkland. That would make two funerals in two weeks, but I found myself deciding to attend.

The other news was that Senator Arlo Devine had announced plans to hold another hearing before the Law and Justice Committee. It was set for next Tuesday in what Senator Devine was now referring to as his "continuing inquiry" into the matter the press was calling the "Capitol Hill Murder."

"Clearly, we need to continue holding some feet to the fire if this thing is going to get resolved," was his assessment. Wilson and his "team" at the Patrol must have been distressed with that news. The last thing they wanted was to spend another wasted morning as a captive audience watching legislators perform for the media.

As I glided down the long I-5 southbound incline into the Nisqually River Basin, I got to thinking about Clive Curtin. I had absolutely no reason to like the man, but he'd showed good sense in discussing the confrontations with the signature gatherers. I was sure he was personally convinced that he and his sports fishing friends were being treated badly by the system. It was hard to know if that might be enough to justify doing whatever was necessary to even the scales, but it didn't seem like it. The only personal threat he faced from Mortenson, based on what I knew, was some embarrassment for writing that foolish letter and letting it become public. None of it was enough reason for him to have murdered the man. How could I be sure?

I was about to pass Nisqually. All I had planned for this morning were a few calls, some bill tracking, and some research in the office. It would only take a moment to ask. I nudged the wheel to the right and headed down the exit ramp.

Norma's Burgers also catered to the breakfast crowd; there were people standing around inside the entrance waiting for a table—a good sign that their Denver omelets were as tasty as their cheeseburgers. The young woman behind the register turned out to have been on duty for breakfast and lunch on the Monday of Senator Mortenson's death. Unfortunately, she didn't remember Clive Curtin.

"He's a big guy, balding, late 50s, early 60s," I told her. "It was the same day I gather you had an accident outside at the intersection there. The guy I'm asking about would probably have been in an expensive suit. Bought a burger with cash."

She laughed at that. "Half the people come through here are in suits. I remember that accident. Awful! But I'm sorry. I haven't got a clue about your guy. Just doesn't ring any bells. I guess you can see how busy we get."

"Would anybody else have waited on him?"

"Nah, would've been me. I do all the takeout stuff here at the counter."

For her trouble, I decided to buy a cup of coffee and a pastry. As she was ringing that up, another question occurred to me. "That same day, also at lunchtime, do you remember selling a burger to a woman, also probably dressed in a nice suit, short dark hair, early thirties, maybe a little exotic looking, always wears scarf and a nice pin."

"You're talking about Paula? Works for the Governor or something?"

"Yeah, Paula McPhee. You know her?"

"Sure. I don't know her last name. But Paula comes in here from time to time. Tips well. She drives a Subaru Crosstrek. Cool car."

That was the right car. It was Paula, all right.

"Day you're asking about," she continued, "she was in here for sure, but she didn't buy anything. Came in looking for someone, and then left. Right after she left was when we all heard the big crash from that accident."

What I'd learned didn't seal things up for Clive Curtin, but it was convincing. He'd probably been right about seeing Paula here that day. I'd pass that tip along to Wilson when I got the chance.

This information got me energized again. My planned quiet morning in the office went out the window. I was letting my work slip, but there was nothing that couldn't wait until tomorrow.

When I arrived at the office I parked in my usual spot in the driveway out front, went inside just long enough to drop off my laptop bag, say "hi" to Helen, and answer a few questions from Janice and our intern. Then, I was back outside on foot headed for the Capitol. I had a few more questions for Judith Bosch.

Judith was at a new workplace upstairs in the Cherberg Building with the rest of the Natural Resources Committee staff. Of all the people I knew, as Mortenson's Legislative Assistant, she was the person most likely to have insights into the man and the people who had dealt with him.

She was happy to help. "Sure, Sandy," she said. "You making any progress in your, uh… investigating?"

"Actually, I'm feeling a bit hopeless about it. I don't really think any of the people I've been talking to probably did it. Don't really know where else to look. I think the State Patrol is stumped as well. Only good news is, they haven't arrested me, at least not yet."

Judith laughed at that. "Well," she said. "I'd like to know who did it, but it isn't the end of the world if we never find out. Knowing what Abel was like, I doubt whoever it was is any kind of risk to anybody else. You're obviously here with some more questions, though. What do you want to know?"

"Well, maybe we could start with Martin Rose," I said. "Did you know the Senator had threatened to complain about Martin to David Prince?"

"Yes, I did. Abel told me that himself."

"Do you think he'd have done that?"

"Oh yeah, in a minute. He didn't like Martin all that much. Thought he was way too full of himself."

"I thought they got along well."

"I'm sure Martin thought that. Abel went out of his way to keep Martin sweet, but Martin has this, I don't know, sort of formal way about him. Abel thought he was pompous and, I don't know, overrated, I guess."

"Martin says he told the Senator he'd pass Curtin's letter along, but that he didn't plan to do it. Do you believe that?"

"Huh. I didn't know that. It does sound like Abel, though. I'm not really sure what Martin would have done. I don't really see what the big deal was. I did exactly the same thing." She stopped to think. "But then, I guess I did get caught at it, didn't I?"

"Only because people started asking questions," I said. "And because it no longer mattered."

"So, if Martin had done like Abel asked, nothing probably would have come of it."

"Not unless the Senator decided to mention *that* to David Prince."

I could see the light dawn. "Oh, I see," she said. "Of course. It would have given Abel leverage."

"Would he have used it?"

"Oh yes. If he'd felt the need, he definitely would have used it."

That's what I thought too. "Okay, so what about our mutual friend, Stephanie? She had some complaints about the Senator as well, right?"

"You're talking about her bill, the public lands for local food thing."

"He didn't want to help her out on that, I gather."

"He was avoiding her. Didn't want to stir up his new Republican buddies about it. But kill him? Nah. Never. Doesn't make any sense at all."

"What I was wondering is whether there might be anything else going on there."

"You don't mean something, I don't know, romantic?"

"Would the Senator have expected more, well, 'return' on his investment. More than she was providing?"

"No. Not what you're thinking, Sandy. Believe me, he'd have expected her political help and support down the road, that's for sure. He was definitely conscious of Stephanie's, um, appeal as a woman. One thing I've got to say about Abel Mortenson, however, is that he was loyal to his wife, Mary. I'm as sure as I could be that he'd never stepped out of line on her. Never that I suspected, anyway. Don't get me wrong. He certainly liked an attractive younger woman, was susceptible, let's say. But, in that one respect, at least, I think he could be counted on for faultless conduct. I think Mary had him totally in hand."

I felt Judith had closed ranks with the other two women, Mary Mortenson and Stephanie Miles, but I tended to trust her perceptions on this. She was certainly a lot closer to all of them than I'd ever been.

Chapter Twenty

Friday, March 12, 9:00 a.m.

The Loyal Constituency

On Friday morning, the commercial fishing industry gathered at the Olympia Red Lion to map out our strategy in opposition to the so-called "Salmon Protection Act" Initiative. The thing was continuing to make headway in signature gathering. Concern about it was mounting while, the murder of Senator Mortenson filled us with uncertainty.

Olympia was a good central meeting place for fishing industry leaders from all over the State. People came from the organizations representing various salmon fishing groups, purse seiners, gillnetters, trollers, and reef netters. They came from as far north as Bellingham, from Port Angeles out on the Olympic Peninsula, from coastal communities out in Westport and South Bend, and from down on the Columbia River. Several of the larger fish processing firms and a couple of the major fisheries supply houses also sent people to attend and assist.

There were also people present from other commercial gear groups, crabbers, trawlers, long-liners, shrimpers, and even some abalone divers. They feared their fisheries were also, indirectly, threatened by this initiative. If the sportsmen pulled this off with salmon, there was every possibility similar efforts could be expected affecting crab, shrimp, cod, and other bottom fish and shellfish.

There were over eighty people gathered in a meeting room for several hours and through lunch. Many of the same people who'd come in for the hearing on Wednesday were back here in Olympia again today. Many were in work clothes and wore baseball caps with advertising for "Detroit Diesel," "Bellingham Cold Storage," or "Seattle Marine Supply." I suppose they may have looked like a rough bunch to the tourists, business travelers, and conference attendees who made up most of the Red Lion clientele. But I knew them to be independent, multi-skilled, capable people who worked very hard for a living in their dangerous, unpredictable, and under-appreciated business. They didn't deserve the grief thrown at them by this initiative.

We roughed out a fund-raising plan, formed a "No on Bogus Initiatives Committee," and appointed some fishing group leaders who would make themselves available to deal with the media and who agreed to be trained in how to do that well. We also heard from three political campaign consulting firms looking to guide us through the coming battle. It was getting serious.

Perhaps most satisfying, many of the old animosities between commercial gear groups faded as we all squared ourselves away to face this common threat.

For me, it was a chance to help my clients in a time of need and to cement important relationships. As the only professional lobbyist actually representing most of them in Olympia and occasionally in D.C., I kept my eye open for new clients as well. I ended up on the Campaign Committee and as head of our External Alliances sub-committee. I'd be leading the effort to secure help from the environmental community, from business leaders and chambers of commerce, and from anyone else who might be sympathetic to our cause. Included as targets for our efforts for support were the Indian Tribes.

I'd given the Tribes a good deal of thought recently. I might have sowed some resentment over my "catch all the non-Tribal 50% share" bill last year and needed to get past that. I believed what Jerry Stockmeyer had told me and still doubted that they'd take a position on the initiative. Even beyond the possible negative public reaction to their involvement in a non-tribal political issue, they might like the measure; it would almost certainly increase their catch.

It would be worth a try, however, to get them to see the logic of opposing it. While the measure would probably not affect Tribal gear, if it passed, they'd end up fishing with gear prohibited for everybody else. That prospect might make them uncomfortable; maybe feeling a bit vulnerable. They knew better than anyone that the gear restrictions the initiative would mandate had nothing whatever to do with how many salmon actually got caught. As nominally neutral participants, and with a voice respected by environmentalists, they could be very helpful in debunking the claim made by the sportsmen that the initiative was about saving salmon. If the Tribes would call it the "baloney" that it was, people would listen. Perhaps we could work with them in some other way even if they wanted to stay mostly behind the scenes.

Despite what Jerry had told me, he still was a good place to start. I'd give him a call to see who among the Tribal Leadership might be the most influential and potentially the least resistant to the idea.

Over lunch, I ended up seated with Dean Miles. Maritime Fisheries Supply was convinced their retail fisheries gear and equipment business would be badly damaged by a significant shift in harvest allocation away from the commercial fleet. They were going to be in this fight for the duration.

"Steph told me to say 'hi,' " he said.

"How's she feeling in her new role as an elected official?"

"Duck to water," he said with a laugh. "She's made for this."

"Her Public Harvest bill looks to be moving."

"She says it's on the Senate Floor. Could be on the Governor's desk early next week."

"Well, give her my congratulations. It's no easy chore getting a bill passed, any bill. She's doing okay for herself as a freshman Representative."

"She has certainly worked for it. For Steph, everything is just a step on the way to success. Who knows, one day I could end up as the Governor's First Gentleman."

Dean was kidding, but only partly. It would be a mistake to underestimate the ambitions of Stephanie Miles.

Chapter Twenty-One

Saturday, March 13, 10:00 a.m.

An Honorary Hiatus

"Dogs," she said.

"Dogs?"

For an answer, the precocious ten-year-old girl who'd come up beside me pointed a chin at the screen of the automatic digital slide-show presentation spooling out before us. "She loved 'em."

We were in the foyer of a Congregational Church in Kirkland next to the sign-in book at Joan Troy's memorial service. After watching a few more pictures cycle through the machine, I saw what the girl meant. There'd been a lot of animals in Joan Troy's life. As a rancher's wife, there were shots of her with cattle, several with young calves and with horses. Mostly, however, wherever this woman had gone and whatever she'd been doing at any given time, there'd been one or more dogs with her or nearby. They were there when she was working on the ranch, when she was out riding, when she was pictured with other members of her family, and even when she was working in the kitchen or relaxing in the comfortable family room of their Okanogan home.

"Dogs," the girl said again, decisively, before nodding and moving off. I didn't have a clue who she was. She walked over and fell into conversation with a group of other well-dressed young mourners. Maybe grandchildren or nieces and nephews or something.

Most of those present today were not here just because Joan Troy's husband was a Washington State Senator. There was another service planned for later, over on the other side of the mountains in Wenatchee. Maybe that one would bring out the local political elite.

The people here today were Joan's childhood friends and family. People she'd known growing up and with whom she'd maintained long-distance relationships over the years. I was impressed by how many people were present. I, too, had fallen under her spell after only the briefest of contacts.

Mostly what impressed me was the contrast between this event and the other service—for Abel Mortenson—I'd attended in Bellingham just a week before.

I've always believed the measure of a man can be seen in the woman he chooses to marry. Joan Troy heightened my respect for her Senator husband. A succession of friends and relatives responded to the invitation to speak of the departed. She'd even made an impression on the Director of the nursing care facility where she'd spent her last few months. She'd had dogs in her life there as well. He spoke passionately about how she'd responded to the dogs provided through a University of Washington Medical School study.

Senator Troy was there, of course. He was thoroughly occupied with offers of condolence and, while I caught his eye at one point, I didn't approach him and add to his burdens.

Chapter Twenty-Two

Monday, March 15, 9:30 a.m.

A Gap in the Record

Early Monday, two weeks after the Senator's death, as I walked over to the Hill for an appointment with a legislator, I texted Paula. She got back to me right away and let me know she was in an early hearing in House Business and Commerce. After my brief appointment, I found her with Aaron Nicolaides near the back of House Hearing Room C. Nicolaides looked spiffy with his dark hair slicked back and in his expensive charcoal suit. He'd definitely traded in his "regular guy" look for something more suitable to his new big business clientele. She was in her usual dark slacks, blouse, colorful scarf, and stylish jacket, looking both businesslike and feminine at the same time. The two of them were far enough toward the back of the long, narrow, mostly-empty hearing room that they could converse, quietly, without disturbing the proceedings. They were definitely having a serious conversation. As I approached, I got an unwelcoming look from Nicolaides, so I shied off, sat down a few rows away to give them some privacy, and occupied myself checking messages on my phone. She knew I was there and wanted to speak with her. I'd catch her when they were done.

It took longer than I'd expected, but after several minutes of discussion, Nicolaides got up and left the room. I went over and took his place.

"You got something in Business and Commerce?" she asked, nodding toward the front of the room.

I laughed. "No," I said. "What about you? You done here?"

She was. We got up and went out into the hall.

"That looked serious," I said, waving my hand back in the direction of where she and Nicolaides had been talking."

"Aaron's great at delegating. Don't think he quite understands I don't still work for him." she said in her typical direct manner.

"Everything oaky?"

"Great, actually. Finally getting some movement."

"You up for coffee?"

She glanced at her phone. "Yeah. How about my office? Don't have a lot of time." Then she smiled. "Coffee's okay, I promise. Russ brought in a Keurig."

She was right. She had her assistant make me a cup of some Hawaiian blend that was as good as anything I'd have gotten at Starbucks.

Her office was nothing special. I guess the assumption is that public servants, especially the ones that work for elected politicians, are supposed to labor away in ascetic surroundings. Maybe it makes some sense. Paula McPhee might not have a seven-foot polished walnut desk and an aniline leather couch in her office, but she does have authority. Her situation was much like some of the young F-18 jet pilots I'd met a few years back during my tour in U.S. Navy JAG. They might have been little more than kids, but the Navy had given them a fifty-million-dollar jet airplane to play with. With the experience she was getting now, Paula was setting herself up nicely for the law firm job I knew she really wanted.

When we were both comfortably seated across her desk with our coffees, I asked, "When we had lunch earlier this week, you mentioned that the day Senator Mortenson died you had a meeting in Seattle at two-thirty?"

"Right?"

"On the way did you, by any chance stop off for lunch at Norma's in Nisqually?"

"Ah, yeah, actually I did. How'd you know that?"

"When you were there, did you happen to see a guy named Clive Curtin? He's in Insurance in Seattle but he's down here a lot. He knows who you are but he doesn't think you know him. He told me he was going in to Norma's when you were coming out."

"No. Don't think I know him. What's he look like?"

"Tall, powerful looking, balding, maybe late fifties. Probably wearing an expensive suit."

She gave that some thought. "No. Can't say I remember anyone in particular. Important?"

"For him, maybe, yeah. That's about the time Senator Mortenson was being murdered. Curtin's also one of our principal opponents in my little 'war' with the sports fishermen. He heads up the campaign committee on their big ballot initiative coming up in November."

"And... he's a potential suspect in this Mortenson thing?

"Yeah."

"Sorry I can't help."

"There was a traffic accident there, at the tip end of Martin Way, at that light right next to Norma's. Did you, by chance, see any of that?"

"Yeah, I did," she said. "Big mess. Got caught up in it. Ended up having to go south on Martin Way, away from the accident. Got back on I-5 north at Marvin Road. Went around it. Lost a lot of time."

"So I guess Curtin's story makes sense."

"Sounds like you wish it didn't."

I laughed. "I guess maybe I do. He's sort of my favorite suspect-candidate."

"Sorry to be unhelpful," she said with a playful smile.

I was thinking about who else might have been on the road to Seattle at that time and remembered Senator Troy's calendar which had been lined out for that Monday afternoon.

"Any chance you saw anyone else you know there at Norma's that day?"

The smile faded. "Um, well, yes," she said after a moment's hesitation. "Also saw Senator Troy. Pulled into the parking lot together; got out of our cars at the same time. Guess you know he's on Ways and Means. Talked briefly by our cars about the budget."

"Really?"

"Yeah. You telling me he's a suspect too?"

"Yeah, I guess he could be. What'd you talk about?"

"Nothing important. No supporter of WWRP. Suppose you can imagine that. Thinks it's just government overreaching. I had what was, for him, some good news. Those of us in the Governor's Office had gone through a lot of soul-searching on WWRP. Given what we faced, the Governor had decided to let the 'Rs' have their WWRP reductions.

I was unhappy about it because it's one of the things we wanted for Fortuna. We hoped it wouldn't be a deal breaker, but it wasn't good. Anyway, I told Troy he might get his WWRP cuts if he could help us out on a couple of other things." She paused a moment. "Not a big deal really."

"Why do you say that?"

"His reaction. I assumed he'd come to Norma's for a burger, like me. When we finished talking, however, he didn't come inside. Instead, got back in his pickup, a big blue king cab with a canopy. Just left. Watched him go as I was getting my purse out of the car. Kind of surprised me."

"Did he get caught up in the accident traffic too?"

She shook her head. "Accident didn't happen till a bit later, after I came back out of Norma's. I was meeting Aaron for lunch. His car wasn't there but I stepped inside anyway to check. Then went back out to my car to wait."

I agreed with her about Troy. It seemed kind of strange that he'd pull in and park there, and then just up and leave without even going inside. "So I guess you saw the accident?" I said.

Once again, she hesitated. "What do you mean?"

"You said it happened after you came back out of Norma's to wait for Aaron."

"Oh, well, yeah. Yeah, I did see some of it, I guess."

"Hit and run, I understand."

"Uh huh."

Again, she was sounding very vague. I was beginning to worry. "You know, Paula, when we had dinner Friday evening, we talked about Norma's Burgers. About your drive to Seattle that day. You never mentioned you'd gone in there. This morning, on the way to work, I stopped in and talked with a young waitress, the one that handles take-out. She doesn't remember Clive Curtin either, but she remembers you." I gave her a smile. "She likes your Crosstrek. Is there something about that stop at Norma's that you're not telling me?"

Her stuffy little office suddenly went very quiet. "Not really relevant to anything," she said.

I just waited.

I could see her making a decision. "Okay, so here's the deal. I did see that accident." She made a face and went silent for a moment. "I'm feeling a bit guilty about it."

"Guilty?" I prompted.

She sighed. "It's like this. I was headed to Seattle, or, actually, Bellevue, to Fortuna's offices that day. Aaron Nicolaides and I agreed to meet there at Nisqually for lunch before the meeting, discuss a few things. I was going to leave my car there, and we'd drive up together in his car."

"Okay," I said.

"So, I checked for him inside and then came back out into the lot to wait. You can see the offramp there from the northbound lanes. I was standing in the lot watching for Aaron's car. It's a big silver Lincoln, a Town Car. At about twenty after twelve, he comes down the off ramp, turns right and comes over toward the traffic light there at the main intersection. I probably haven't mentioned it, but he's a terrible driver. He drinks. Hardly even paused at the stop sign at the end of the off-ramp. Then, when he got over to the light, it was still red. He just blasted right through in a big sweeping right turn onto Martin Way.

"This little brown Toyota was coming off the overpass from the Southbound exit. Maybe going a little fast, but not really. Probably wanted to make the light. Aaron pulled right in front of it. Toyota swerved left and ended up in a head-on with another car that was coming the other way through the light toward the northbound on ramp. Both of them wanting to make the green light. Awful crash. There were apparently some really bad injuries. Aaron's car wasn't even touched. He obviously saw it happen; he stopped maybe a couple hundred feet or so up Martin Way. Paused there for a bit. Then just drove on. Instead of turning in and meeting up as we'd planned, he went on up Martin Way to the south and disappeared."

"Are you sure it was him? Lots of Town Cars around."

"Of course, it was him. Well, I mean the thing has tinted windows; I didn't see the driver. But how many of those silver Town Cars are there? He never showed up at Norma's. I waited for quite a while just in case. I ended up driving to the meeting on my own. He was there when I arrived."

"What did he say about it?"

"Said he got caught in the stalled traffic waiting to exit off of I-5 and just decided to skip it and meet me in Bellevue instead. Said he called, but I didn't get any call. That Town Car had to have been him."

"So, this is why you didn't want to talk about your stop at Norma's that day?"

"Jesus, Sandy, he damn near killed those people. Came out without a scratch, himself. I'm willing to bet he'd been drinking, at least some. I feel horrible about not reporting it."

"Why didn't you?" But as I asked the question, I guessed the answer.

She looked miserable with guilt. "I should have. But, Jesus Sandy, I can't make the man an enemy. When he stopped, I bet he wasn't more than fifty yards from where I was standing by my car in Norma's parking lot. He could have seen me. I was in plain view. Instead he just drove off and pretended he'd never been there. What a shit! What does that make me for not reporting him? Probably an even worse shit."

"I guess it's understandable, Paula, but you should say something."

"I know. I got to the meeting and there he was working the room. All calm and normal. Hundreds of millions of dollars at stake. What was I supposed to do? Longer I waited, the harder it got. You know they've offered me a job?"

"Fortuna?"

"The Morganthau Firm. In their business and government relations department. I'd be working with Aaron. Come in as a partner." She laughed bitterly. "At this point I can call that history."

Morganthau, Staley, and Rimes was the perfect firm for her. It employed several hundred lawyers. Its practice included insurance defense, a strong land use management department, several Northwest Indian Tribes, and, most important for Paula, a serious business practice with some of the largest firms in the Pacific Northwest. They had offices in seven Western states and in Washington, D.C. It was exactly what she wanted; it was her dream. The very idea of such a job turned my stomach inside out. I was delighted for her, however. She probably knew there was almost certainly an implicit condition on that job offer: success on the Fortuna Package.

"I do think you're going to need to say something, Paula. About seeing the accident. I'd call Lieutenant Nathan Wilson with the State Patrol. Tell him I sent you. He'll put you on to the right person. You should tell them everything we've talked about. I'm really sorry I had to be the one to bring all this up."

"I know. You're right." She shook her head in frustration. "I'll make the call."

Chapter Twenty-Three

Monday, March 15, 10:30 a.m.

Dead Letter

C all she did. I discovered that, because it wasn't more than half an hour later that Lieutenant Wilson called me. He wanted to see me back in his office "as soon as possible."

This whole Mortenson thing was throwing my regular paying client work off track. Too many late nights at work. As I headed over to the State Patrol office, I got a welcome text from Senator Fang's Legislative Assistant letting me know that Fang had, in fact, turned down Clive Curtin's "sport priority" bill for executive session. That effectively put it to bed, at least for this Session. Our gillnet-bird bill had finally passed the Senate and was headed to Governor Browne for signature. That was good news for some very worried fishermen. The pressure was off, and in record time. I had some other stuff to track and work, but my next big push would probably come this summer and fall, over the ballot initiative. Assuming the sports guys got their signatures and it qualified for the ballot.

The fact that I had some time to spare didn't prevent me feeling uneasy about my meeting with Wilson. I figured Wilson might give me hell for continuing to investigate the case by questioning Paula. Resigned to my fate, I headed over to the State Patrol office in the General Admin Building again, made my presence known to the officer on the desk, and took a seat to wait.

And wait.

I didn't have a specific appointment, but I was there at Wilson's request, so it was perturbing to be cooling my heels for nearly three-quarters of an hour.

Initially, I thumbed through a battered collection of "gun-and-ammo," "car-and-driver," and "modern policing" magazines. They were all older issues; personal second-hand cast-offs from individual State employees who probably worked there in the State Patrol office. There is a weird, arcane twist in the Washington State Constitution that prohibits the State from "lending its credit." So, State agencies can't apparently hold magazine subscriptions because they inevitably have to be paid in advance. The State of Washington *never* pays in advance. The mixed and battered collection of second-hand waiting room magazines was not atypical in reception areas of State government. As silly and inconvenient as this was, it was just one more demonstration how government, presumably reflecting its citizens' wishes, can sometimes be unbelievably cheap.

Anyway, I got tired of the magazines and, as I came to realize I might be in for an even longer wait, I started tracking a few bills on my phone and scrolling through the Legislative webpage for current news. There was a list of Governor Browne's actions earlier that morning on several bills that had landed on his desk. It was way too soon for my gillnet-bird bill, but I was curious anyway. Most of them I wasn't familiar with—like new penalties for cyber-crimes and tighter requirements for pleasure boat licenses. Legislatures deal with an incredible variety of issues.

But, there was another bill, one that Browne had apparently vetoed entirely. It caught my eye because of its title and because of something I'd heard at Joan Troy's service on Saturday morning in the brief eulogy from the Director of her care facility. The bill was titled: "Prohibiting the use of public dollars for dogs and other pets for patients under medical care." It had been prime-sponsored by Senator Gerald Potter, which was enough in itself to explain its likely purpose. Potter was one of those legislators who just couldn't help but pander to a tax-sensitive public over any appropriation that could, somehow, however lame the argument, be made to look bad. The Potters of this world were why there'd never be, at least in my lifetime, current magazines in any office of Washington State government.

This particular bill had originated out of a TV news special report, one of the so-called "Flash Reports" they liked to title: "Your Tax Dollars at Work." They were all about "waste, fraud, and abuse."

I hadn't connected it when I'd heard that eulogy. Now I remembered that report a few weeks back. The segment had been titled: "Can Rover Cure Cancer?" That had been followed by the lead: "Washington State's premier university is providing free pets for indigent cancer, Alzheimer's, and other patients, according to a recent report from the University of Washington Medical School. 'The dogs seem to make them feel better,' said a source close to the program. The study is funded by a $350,000 grant from the National Institutes of Health and by the University's School of Medicine." That had been followed by a thoroughly uncharitable account of why this "so-called research" was idiotic and wasteful.

A budget hawk like Gerald Potter could never resist a media gift like that. He'd apparently enlisted an impressive cadre of Republicans and several Democrats to join him as co-sponsors. All of them would, no doubt, cite the bill in the coming election as a proof of their fiscal responsibility. Just to make sure the legislators on the bill were thoroughly noticed for their support, after the bill had passed a few days earlier, there'd been a follow-up report in which the station offered that action as evidence of the "impact" of its hard-charging investigative reporting.

They'd jumped the gun, however. Things had changed.

I watched the Governor's veto message online. He'd commented: "I am reversing my previously announced decision to sign this bill. Upon further consideration, I've concluded such a veto would disrupt valuable research already funded and underway. It would place currently outstanding grant funding in question. This research is costing Washington taxpayers next to nothing. It is almost entirely paid for by out-of-state resources, bringing much needed revenue into our state and creating jobs here that would, otherwise, go elsewhere. Moreover, from all reports I've heard, this groundbreaking University of Washington effort is already extending lives and providing some remarkable results."

As I read those details, several pieces of the puzzle I'd struggled with over the past two weeks suddenly fell into place. To confirm, I called the Secretary of the Senate's office and inquired about their records that document member votes and attendance.

Then I knew.

It was nearly eleven when Wilson finally came into the waiting room from his office. "I think I know who did it," were the first words out of my mouth.

That caught his attention.

"And, I think I know where you can find the proof."

Wilson gave me a look over the top of his reading glasses and then just waved for me to follow him down the hall.

Moments later we were in his office with the door closed. "Okay, spill it, Dalton."

"I think it was Senator Troy," I said before either of us had a chance to sit. Then I poured out all my thinking in a single rush. "His wife had Alzheimer's. She was a lifelong dog lover. She was getting pet therapy through a UW research study using dogs. The therapy was working. Troy killed Mortenson so the Democrats would take over and thus allow the Governor to veto a bill that will kill that study. It was vetoed this morning, too late to help Troy's wife, but he couldn't have known that. Last Monday, Troy was headed for Seattle just after noon. He'd cancelled his afternoon calendar so he could visit his wife. He changed his mind and came back to the Capitol after learning something important in a conversation he had at Nisqually with Paula McPhee. He knew that security camera was on the blink. His office is just at the foot of the steps. He keeps a change of clothes in his office and I'd bet there's still blood splatter evidence on something in one of his bags."

I was a little breathless. I probably looked slightly crazy to the disciplined and methodical Lieutenant. But, to his credit more than mine, he waved me to a chair and sat behind his desk. "Okay, Mr. Dalton," he said. Let's start at the beginning. Where is all this coming from?"

I spelled it all out. About Digger Troy's wife and her lifelong love for dogs. About the UW Pet Therapy Study and the bill that would have ended it. About Troy's dislike for Mortenson's politics, particularly the pandering to the Indian Tribes, and Troy's resentment when Mortenson took Troy's coveted Chair on Natural Resources.

Based on its subject matter and the amazing list of sponsors, the bill had been all but a sure thing for passage. It had support from both sides of the aisle. The relevant Committee Chairs were on board. Even after the shift to Democratic control caused by Mortenson's death, it had still passed; the new Democratic Chair of Senate Higher Education Committee had been one of the bill's co-sponsors. The capper: The

Governor had publicly agreed to sign it.

That bill had been a done deal.

On the Monday of Mortenson's death, Troy had cancelled his afternoon appointments and, as he'd already done on a couple of previous occasions this session, he'd headed for Seattle to spend the rest of the day with his ailing wife at her nursing care facility there. On the way, he'd stopped off to grab something for lunch at Norma's Burgers in Nisqually. There, in the parking lot, he'd run into Paula. Paula was leading the Governor's effort to pass the Fortuna incentives package.

One of those incentives was an appropriation for the WWRP program that was larger than the Republicans wanted, an appropriation that Troy, in particular, a Member of Ways and Means, was actively opposing. Paula told Troy that the Governor had decided to conditionally agree to the Republican position on WWRP and was willing if necessary, to cut the appropriation well below what Troy knew the Governor wanted.

That was the moment Troy suddenly understood what he needed to do.

He knew that if the Democrats had been in the majority in the Senate, there was no way the Governor would have agreed to that reduced WWRP appropriation. He instantly appreciated that the exact same thing would be true for other bills as well, bills the Governor would, reluctantly, be willing to sign in exchange for Republican concessions on Fortuna. But, only because of the Republican Senate majority. The 'no pets for patients' bill was one of those bills. Troy knew beyond question that, if given the chance, Governor Browne, a liberal Democrat, would absolutely prefer to veto that bill. As long as Republicans were in charge, however, a veto would just drive another nail in the coffin of his Fortuna Package. Browne couldn't do it.

Burning with grief over his wife's painfully tragic decline, Digger Troy changed his plans. Instead of continuing on to Seattle that Monday, after he'd spoken with Paula he'd returned to the Newhouse Building. Before he'd left, Troy had seen Mortenson heading back up the stairs with a cup of coffee just after noon so he knew the man would be there. Returning to his own office, Troy had then walked up the back stairway to Mortenson's office knowing about the disabled security camera. He'd killed Mortenson with the Indian hunting knife so proudly and disingenuously displayed on Mortenson's desk.

Then, after calmly wiping his prints off the knife with the Senator's own tie that was laying on his desk, Troy had exited the room and the office, slipped back down the stairs to his own office directly beneath. There, after possibly changing at least some of his clothing which might have been splattered with blood, he simply went back to work, attended his afternoon hearing and then the late afternoon Floor Session. That evening he drove back to Seattle as usual for his evening visit with his wife.

The ultimate proof of Troy's commission of this crime could very possibly still be contained in either the overnight bag or in the garment bag that hung by the sofa in his office right there in the Newhouse Building.

"I don't know, Dalton. We're going to need a search warrant. What do I tell the Judge? 'He killed her because his wife liked dogs, your honor.' " Wilson shook his head doubtfully. "The whole thing's pretty damn thin."

At my encouragement, Wilson called the Lady of the Lamp Nursing Care facility in Seattle and confirmed that Joan Troy, a patient at their facility had died last Thursday evening. They were reticent to provide more detailed patient information, but Wilson got the Director on the line. At my urging, he gave me the phone and then put it on speaker so he could overhear.

"I wanted to tell you how much I appreciated your comments at Joan Troy's service on Saturday." I told him. "I found them very inspiring."

"She was a wonderful woman," he replied. "She will definitely be missed."

"I'm here with Lieutenant Nathan Wilson at the State Patrol. He's looking into another matter and I told him you might be able to fill us in on that University of Washington pet therapy research you mentioned in your talk?"

"That program's amazing," he said. "Worked wonders for our patients here. We couldn't believe it when we read about that bill that would kill it. Joan Troy's husband, the Senator, was incensed about it. Here we had something that was really working, and they want to just kill it. Nonsense. Absolute nonsense."

"So, you must have been glad to hear about the Governor's veto."

"You're right about that. He won a few votes around this place with that veto, I can tell you." He chuckled. "I hope Senator Troy comes in for some credit. I bet he gave the Governor an earful. He was damn angry about it; I can tell you that. Joan Troy loved those dogs and they did her a world of good in return."

When Wilson heard that, I could tell from his look that he was taking my argument a lot more seriously. After we ended the call he gave what he'd heard a moment of silent consideration. Then he got back on the phone and, this time, called Paula McPhee.

"When we spoke, earlier today," he told her, "you mentioned being at Norma's in Nisqually last Monday?"

"Yeah, that's right," she said. "I told your colleague everything I could recall about that accident. Sorry I don't know that guy Curtin. But I was there, all right. So, if he saw me, he must have been there too."

"I have another question, Ms. McPhee. While you were there, I understand from Sandy Dalton that you also ran into Senator Troy. Out in the parking lot, I believe?"

"Yeah, that's right, Lieutenant. Like I told Sandy, Senator Troy was interested in the WWRP appropriation. I told him about the Governor's decision to reconsider his position on the Republican cuts to WWRP if he could get some help with our Fortuna legislation. He seemed pleased by that, but I thought his reaction to it was kind of strange."

"How do you mean, Ms. McPhee?"

"Well, like you said, we ran into each other out in the parking lot. He'd just driven in there and got out of his truck near where I was just getting out of my car. When we finished talking, instead of going inside to get lunch or something, Troy just got back in his truck and left. Went over to I-5 and took the southbound on-ramp back toward Olympia. You can see the whole area from there. It just seemed strange to me. He drove all the way out there and then just turned around and went back without getting lunch."

When he hung up from talking with Paula, I could tell Wilson was even more convinced. I watched as he now thought over what she had told him.

Then he reached out and made yet another call. This one was to Senator Troy's Legislative Assistant who, with a senior State Patrol officer on the phone, quickly and willingly confirmed that, at around eleven on the Monday of Mortenson's death Senator Troy had, indeed, asked her to cancel all his afternoon appointments because he needed to drive to Seattle.

"When I got back from lunch, however," she said. "He was right here, working in his office as usual. He attended the afternoon Committee Hearing as well as a late afternoon Session on the Senate Floor. Said he just changed his mind.

When he ended the call with Senator Troy's Assistant, it was obvious Wilson had reached a decision. He immediately called in Hughes and directed him to go over and post himself in the Newhouse Building hallway just outside Senator Troy's office. If Troy or anyone else came out of that office with any luggage, an overnight bag, a garment bag, or anything that looked like it might contain clothing, Hughes was to either secure permission to see what they were carrying or, if necessary, secure the unopened bag and reman there with it until the warrant arrived.

This was a huge relief. Troy had not been present at his office when Wilson had spoken with the Legislative Assistant but I was sure she'd catch up with him wherever he was and tell him about Wilson's call. It had been two weeks since the murder so it was entirely possible that any bloodied clothes in those bags would be long gone by now. If not, however, one wouldn't want to give Troy a chance to dispose of them before a search warrant could be served. Fortunately, Wilson wasn't just an empty uniform. Even if he'd been slow to come around, it seemed he finally felt he had enough to justify that warrant.

This was, however, still a Washington State Senator's Capitol Campus office they were about to search. Wilson needed to speak with his Chief.

I was asked to stand by back out in the lobby while Wilson drafted up the warrant application. While I waited, I was to write out my 'statement' in detail on a form provided by the State Patrol, sign it under oath, and then have the officer at the desk deliver it back to the Lieutenant. Then and only then, with my statement, his statement, and his draft application in hand, he'd call on the Chief for approval to secure the warrant.

It was all so painfully cumbersome. Even with an officer standing in the hall outside the office, I could still picture Senator Troy somehow disposing of the guilty evidence, maybe sneaking it out in a briefcase.

I waited there anxiously for at least another hour.

It was nearly one when Wilson finally came back into the waiting room. "Fitzroy has the warrant," he said. "You stay put. I don't want you screwing this up." Then, as he was stepping out the door on his way across campus to the Newhouse Building he turned. "I hope you're right," he said."

So did I.

For yet another hour I sat in that cold, molded-plastic chair and waited. The smattering of outdated magazines provided little relief. As the time passed, increasingly all I could think about was how big a mistake this would be if I turned out to be wrong. I would make a bitter enemy of a powerful State Senator, one whose help my clients needed. I would cause what could become a public embarrassment for the State Patrol, for its Chief, and, tragically, for one Lieutenant Nathan Wilson, a man I was beginning to respect.

As I awaited Wilson's return, that afternoon, I couldn't help wondering what the hell I'd been thinking to have put myself in this god-awful situation.

Chapter Twenty-Four

Monday, March 15, 2:00 p.m.

Failed Motion of Censure

It was nearly two when Wilson and his team passed back through the waiting room at State Patrol Headquarters. I knew immediately from their look that things had not gone well. Fitzroy and Hughes carried what appeared to be the two travel bags I'd seen in Troy's office the week before and the big appointment book from the Assistant's desk. They lugged it all through reception and into the back office area, while Wilson came over to me.

"Nothing," he said with a grim headshake. "Change of clothes. Shaver. Toothbrush. Soap. We'll send it out for trace analysis, but the clothing all looks clean and unworn as far as we can see. Senator's Assistant says the bags haven't been moved for nearly a month."

I didn't know what to say to that, so I said nothing.

"Why don't you call it a day, Dalton," Wilson said with a deep sigh. "Nothing more for you to do here. Maybe something will turn up in the lab report."

With that, he too disappeared into the back offices. The whole thing seemed so anti-climactic I couldn't help feeling both disappointed and like I had somehow let Wilson down. I left the State Patrol office, made the long walk across campus back to my office, and after hearing a brief bill status report from Helen, I retreated to my upstairs office, closed the door, and hibernated behind my computer.

I'd always thought Troy was a good man. If it turned out I was wrong about this, I was going to feel very bad.

I'd been so sure they'd find bloody clothing in those bags that it threw me to learn that it had all looked clean and unworn. Something could still turn up in a lab report. It was also possible that Troy hadn't even worn those clothes or that he hadn't been splattered with blood in the first place. I also, however, had to face the very real possibility that I'd gotten the whole thing completely wrong. The more I thought about it, I couldn't let go of the very real possibility that I'd screwed this up, that I was misinterpreting what I knew, and that I'd probably just made a very serious enemy of Senator Digger Troy, a man my clients needed in their ongoing battles here in the Legislature. The idea of it nagged at me. I couldn't let it go. As a result, I found myself reconsidering what I knew.

I had to wonder: if it wasn't Troy, who had it been? If it was, perhaps there was something else I already knew that could prove it.

There was the murder itself: Mortenson had been killed, perhaps symbolically, with an antique Native American hunting knife. That seemed consistent with Senator Troy's anti-tribal views. But he wasn't the only one for whom that might make sense. The crime might have been either premeditated or committed in the heat of the moment, probably the latter. There was the lengthy window of opportunity, between just after noon when I'd left, until about one twenty-five when Judith Bosch had, apparently, returned. Several of those factors made sense for Troy, but none of them really excluded other suspects either.

None of the many known suspects, other than Troy, in my now questionable judgment, really had a sufficiently powerful motive to kill. Of course, there was the fact that the field of additional potentially motivated suspects, ones we could only guess at, was also quite large. That wasn't just because so many people disliked Abel Mortenson. It was also because a great many people might have benefited from his death.

In my frustration, I pulled up on my computer the notes I'd typed up on the statements by the various witnesses and suspects I'd interviewed over the past week. None of it led anywhere.

Then I scanned the crime scene report that I'd been given that day last week in Wilson's office.

That was where I noticed something that, initially, just seemed unusual. The more I considered it, the more startling and horrible it became.

I couldn't believe what I was reading. It couldn't be true.

How could I have possibly been so wrong?

With a huge lump in the pit of my stomach, and mindful of the time, I hurried back downstairs, made a quick excuse to Helen for my erratic conduct, and went out to my car.

The Thurston County Courthouse was on the hillside just above the far shore of Capitol Lake. It was a longer drive there from my office than you might think. And this day it was a frustrating drive. Instead of going through town, I tried to avoid the lights and traffic by going the long way around, using I-5 and Highway 101. I ended up behind some mid-day oversized vehicle tow consisting of three segments of a modular home that had traffic creeping along most of the way while I indulged my life-long weakness for silent and not-so-silent curses.

The whole way there my mind swirled with questions. If what I suspected was correct, I'd be living down that misfired search of Senator Troy's office for some time to come and my own life was about to turn upside down. Finally, at the Office of the Thurston County Court Clerk, I did a search through their indexes and court records. I'd come here in person because not everything is on line and I wanted a filing clerk's help to be absolutely certain I didn't miss something.

Many court and other records are also kept on a statewide online archive maintained by the Washington Secretary of State with cooperation from local counties or on the various county websites. While I was there, I took a seat in the visitor area at the Clerk's Office and used my phone to look at some of the records for Skagit County and King County as well, just to be sure.

When that was done, I had my answer; not the one I was hoping for. I'd been a fool in every way imaginable. Even then, I was still desperately hoping I was wrong.

Chapter Twenty-Five

Monday, March 15, 3:00 p.m.

Vote on Final Passage

I t was three by the time I got back, parked my car, and made my way over to the second floor of the Cherberg building to Judith Bosch's new workplace at the Natural Resources Committee office. On the way, I'd called ahead to be sure she'd be there. I needed to ask this question in person. When I arrived, I was surprised to find her at her desk in close conversation with Stephanie Miles. Mortenson's death had pulled the two of them closer in their long-standing friendship.

"Judith, I have a quick question. Do you mind if I interrupt?"

They obviously didn't mind at all. Stephanie got up to go, but I waved at her to stay; she might be able to help.

With that, I quietly asked two questions and got exactly the two answers I'd feared. Both Judith Bosch and Stephanie Miles were very sure. Both had good reason to know, better than anyone in Abel Mortenson's life outside of his wife.

That was all I needed. I excused myself and headed back down the stairs and outside. Then, all but running, I hurried on foot back across Campus to the State Patrol Office, hoping I could manage the next critical challenge.

I had to see the actual evidence.

Lieutenant Wilson was in a meeting. I was, however, able to catch Officer Fitzroy, the slightly more senior of the Fitzroy & Hughes duo. He was also, I thought, the more approachable of the two. He did not, however, look happy to see me. I'd obviously made no friends at the State Patrol today.

"Look, I'm really sorry to bother you," I said apologetically. "But something further has come up. There's something I need to know."

Officer Fitzroy looked skeptical.

"I need to look at the crime scene evidence," I said. I held up a hand: "Just the necktie. All I need is a look. I won't touch a thing. Just let me take a look."

"Mr. Dalton," he began, "don't you think you've ought to leave this to us..."

I didn't even let him continue. "I know," I said. "Believe me, I do know how strange this seems, given what you've just been through with the search and everything. I believe, however, that I finally know what really happened. I need to be sure before I take it further. I think it could be urgent. I guess I could call the Lieutenant out of his meeting. If I'm wrong, that's going to turn out to be a big waste of time.

"All I need, Officer Fitzroy," I pleaded, "is a quick look at that necktie. The one you folks found at the scene of Mortenson's murder."

Perhaps, among themselves, Fitzroy, Hughes, and Wilson hadn't been as convinced of my guilt as I'd feared. Perhaps Fitzroy was also thinking he didn't want me to needlessly disturb his boss in whatever meeting he was in. Maybe he was even slightly intimidated by the extent to which the Lieutenant and I had been working together over the past couple of days. Whatever his reasons, he turned away without another word and disappeared back down the hallway leading to the interior of the complex. For a moment, I wondered if he'd just abandoned me there in complete disgust. But, to my huge relief, a few moments later he reappeared carrying a common 'bankers box" with "Mortenson, Abel," written on it along with the date of death, a case number, and some other incomprehensible information.

"Just look. No touch!" he said with a scowl as he opened the box.

He reached in and pulled out a clear plastic zip-lock bag containing an obviously bloodstained, red cotton tie with a tiny, barely visible insignia from the maker stitched into its center.

Oh, Christ! I thought. I took a deep breath. "Can you turn it over, let me see the label?" I asked, my stomach in turmoil.

He did so. The easily recognizable, slightly frayed label bore a small check mark in permanent black ink that had been there since the day, a year earlier, when it had been purchased on sale at Nordstrom's Rack in downtown Seattle.

I knew that for sure for a very good reason: I was the person who had purchased it.

That necktie was mine.

Chapter Twenty-Six

Monday, March 15, 3:10 p.m.

A Late Addition to the Agenda

I t was only very reluctantly that Officer Fitzroy finally complied with my urgent plea, pushed the button on the Patrol's ancient intercom at the reception desk, and interrupted Lieutenant Wilson's meeting. It wasn't until a few moments later that I appreciated just why he'd been so slow to do so. That only became clear to me after he'd led me up a stairway and then down to the end of a long, polished hall where we'd stopped before the door of what looked to be an impressive office and on which he'd made a gentle, respectful knock.

That's when I saw the gold lettering on the door that read: "Lehan K. Orbison, Jr., Chief."

Thoroughly intimidated, I stepped through that door into a bright, corner office with a very large desk behind which sat the Chief of the Washington State Patrol, the man I'd seen testifying in the Law and Justice Committee hearing the previous week. Seated in front of the desk was Wilson and another man, an Assistant Chief, whom I hadn't met. All of them, including Chief Orbison, were in uniform. None of them stood.

"The man of the hour," said Wilson, ironically. "Chief, this is Sandy Dalton. Dalton, Chief Orbison. This is my immediate boss, Chief Saylor." As I shook hands, I noticed the door being pulled softly closed from the outside as Fitzroy tactfully, and maybe also tactically, withdrew.

What the hell had I gotten myself into?

There was an empty chair and Wilson waved at it as Chief Orbison was, saying: "Mr. Dalton, why don't you tell us what you apparently told the Lieutenant last week. About how Senator Mortenson's death will affect the Legislature?"

Apparently, they'd been discussing me. Wilson had presumably been trying to explain to his bosses why there could be such a multitude of possible motives for the Mortenson murder. He wouldn't have been in here doing that unless they were dissatisfied with his performance. So, I wouldn't be here unless Wilson was in trouble.

Orbison did not look like a happy man. All of them, including Orbison, had to be under a lot of pressure. The tension between them was palpable. They would all be painfully aware that, tomorrow morning, they'd be back in front of the TV cameras answering more questions from Senator Arlo Devine, from the "deeply concerned" members of his Law and Justice Committee, and later, in the hall, from the press. This time around, they'd not only have little or nothing to report, they could also could count on being publicly grilled about the disastrous Troy search—for which I was obviously responsible.

Justified or not, that search was going to look very much like an amateurish mistake—one where the police had jumped the gun on a questionable warrant. Wilson's particular misfortune was that it was a mistake which seemed painfully similar to the one Al Borichevsky had told me about; the mistake Orbison himself had so visibly made just a few years earlier in that press-worthy I-90 hit-and-run investigation. No doubt it now looked to Orbison like his subordinate was about to embarrass him a second time over a misplaced search. Only this time it was Wilson's screw up. Surely Orbison wasn't going to let *that* pass.

I was betting that my being brought in here hadn't been Wilson's idea at all. It had probably been the Chief's.

Now, however, the whole discussion of who might have had motive was no longer relevant. I knew who'd committed this crime. Those lab results were going to come back negative because Senator Troy was innocent. If this case was going to get solved before tomorrow morning's Law and Justice hearing, these guys needed to get moving.

"Chiefs. Lieutenant," I said. I was still a little breathless from my haste to get over here. I was still processing what I had discovered. Did I really want to tell them what I'd learned? I was deeply troubled by what I was about to say… but I said it anyway: "With all due respect, I've just learned something that makes all that moot. I think I know what happened in this murder, and it has nothing at all to do with the Legislature, or with Senator Troy."

Wilson leaned back in his chair, took a deep breath and then let out a long, slow exhale as if bringing himself under control. Chief Saylor turned toward Wilson with a look that said: "Who the hell is this guy?"

Chief Orbison just looked surprised. "Jesus, Dalton," he said. "You can't be serious?"

"I am, believe me. I was just out there in your front office. Officer Fitzroy was kind enough to show me the bloody necktie your CSI people recovered from the Mortenson crime scene. I'm not sure how to tell you this, but, well, I interrupted your meeting because that necktie…"

"Yes?"

I still hesitated. Then: "Well… it's mine."

For a moment, the room went deathly silent. A car passed on the street outside the window. Then Wilson, shaking his head, said: "Yours…? Yours? You're talking about the tie we found at the scene. The one the killer used to wipe off the murder weapon?"

I also let out breath in a long, slow puff of air. All three of them were staring at me intently, obviously incredulous. "Exactly." I said finally. "My tie, red cotton, Vermont Mills. Has a black check mark on the label from when it was marked down at Nordstrom's where I bought it a year or so ago. There isn't any doubt. None. I recognize it and can swear it's mine."

Wilson was shaking his head. Again, they were all momentarily speechless. Then Wilson became the first with anything to say to that. "All right, Dalton. I need to inform you, you have a right to remain silent. Anything you say…"

I held up my hand to interrupt. "I know all that, Lieutenant. I hasten to add, I did *not* kill the man, but that *is* my tie. So, what you've got to be asking is, how did it get there?"

Wilson made to continue, but Chief Orbison stopped him. "Let's just hold on, here," he said. "This all needs to be handled properly." He pointed out his door and down the hall. "Lieutenant, why don't you take Dalton, go back to work, and get to the bottom of this. There's no need for Chief Saylor and I to be involved." He was shaking his head and holding up his hands in a way that suggested to me that it was more like he didn't *want* to be involved. "It's your investigation. Why don't you just go ahead and get on with it."

As we left Orbison's office and Wilson escorted me back down the hall, he gave me a look that said: "Boy have you got yourself into it now!" I knew it wasn't just me—it was his career at stake here as well.

For a second time, I was relieved not to be taken to an official interview room. Once we were back seated in his office, Wilson did start things off by insisting on reading me my rights. When he'd finished and I'd waived them, he said: "Okay, to start with "what you're saying just doesn't make any damn sense. You say that's your tie. There was only the one tie found at that scene. Mortenson wasn't wearing one. I'm told he always had a tie. So, if that was *your* tie, where the hell is *his*?"

"The killer must have taken it."

Wilson obviously found this whole situation unbelievable. He seemed at a loss for words. Finally he said, "Yeah, that or you've just remembered you left it there and are looking for a way out."

He was right, of course. "Look, Lieutenant," I said. "You know I didn't do this. I had absolutely no motive; on the contrary, I needed the man alive. And I really didn't have an opportunity' you know the Senator was alive and well when I left his office that day. Yeah, I could have come back later, but why the hell would I have done that? Moreover, I sure as hell wouldn't be here telling you any of this if I had something to hide."

He looked at me long and hard. "What a mess," he finally said, shaking his head yet again.

"There's something else you need to know," I said. It didn't look like Wilson really wanted to hear it. He listened anyway. "According to Judith Bosch, Mortenson *never* wore a red tie, and never cotton. He hated red ties. All his ties were silk. They were always blue. Plain, with no design. So, for that reason too, that tie wasn't his. Except when he was working alone in the office, he always wore a tie. There's no way around it; the killer has to have removed Mortenson's tie and left mine behind to replace it."

Wilson seemed totally confused. He said nothing. He just waited for me to continue.

"Lieutenant, I'm well aware how all this probably sounds. This time I'm reasonably certain I know exactly who the killer is. I think I know how you can prove it. With any luck, you could make an arrest before this day is over."

This stopped Wilson cold. Solving the case before tomorrow's hearing had to be a big motivator. Then his native pessimism set in. He made a cynical face. "This time…" he said, sardonically.

"I know, Lieutenant. It hasn't been a good day. Even so, everything I told you earlier today proved to be true. I'd just drawn the wrong conclusions. So, let me suggest what I think are the right ones."

Wilson had to know that without Senator Troy, he had nothing. The man in that big office down the hall wasn't going to be patient forever. Not with half the State watching and with the Patrol having nothing to say at tomorrow's hearing.

"Okay, Dalton," he said. "I'm listening. Lay it out. Ten minutes. Make it good."

So, I did, and it was.

While it took more than ten minutes, by the time I was done I could tell that Wilson was convinced.

"Stay put," he said, pointing a very long index finger at my chair.

Then he went back out into the hall pulling a small notebook out of his pocket and went, I believe, into the office next door. I could hear him talking to Fitzroy and Hughes, giving them instructions, but it was hard to tell what he was saying. Finally, he came back out into the hall and I heard him saying: "If they're unwilling to come, convince them. We're getting this thing done, and we're doing it today."

With that, he stepped back into his office where I sat waiting. "Okay Dalton," he said. "Here's where you make yourself useful. You think Aaron Nicolaides is around the Capitol today?"

"It's a pretty good bet. He was here this morning."

"Think you could find him and get him in here?"

"Don't know. I can sure try."

"I've got Fitzroy and Hughes rounding up several of our witnesses over the next hour or so, but I also want to have a chat with Nicolaides. You find him. You just tell him that I need to talk with him about the murder and that I'd like to see him here at headquarters. Nothing more. ASAP. Make it routine, but make sure he gets here, Okay? If possible, sometime in the next half-hour, forty-five minutes or so."

"Sure Lieutenant. I'm on my way." With that, I headed down the hall toward the exit and pulled out my phone. I didn't have Nicolaides in my contacts list, but I was sure he'd be a member of the Third House.

They'd have his cell number over in the Gulch and even, maybe, know where he was.

I caught up with Aaron Nicolaides in person, just before he walked in to an appointment with a House Member up on the fourth floor of the O'Brien Building. He was impressed with a request from the State Patrol and was willing enough to come. He wasn't about to walk away from an important appointment, however. It would only be brief, so I told him where to come and rested on what seemed to be his sincere promise to head over as soon as he had the chance.

By the time I was back at Patrol Headquarters, Wilson had, apparently, commandeered what looked to be a modest-sized conference room. I was directed there by the officer at reception and found Wilson straightening up chairs and lining up a pen and note pad at a place just to the left of the head of the table. The second-floor room was on the west side of the building with a view across Capitol Lake. It wasn't your standard interrogation cubicle; it was more like a modest conference room. It did seem to be equipped with video recording equipment. It looked like it would be serving double duty as an interrogation room. I hadn't yet seen anything that looked like a holding cell, either. These offices at the Capitol seemed to be more administrative than anything else. They probably didn't question a lot of suspects here.

Wilson motioned to me to enter. "Nicolaides?" he asked.

"He was just going in for an appointment with a legislator. He should be here in another half hour or so. Seemed completely willing. I felt like an idiot waiting around for him, I hope that was all right."

He just nodded.

I looked around the room. Obviously, Wilson was getting things set up to gather the final details from our witnesses and try to wind this thing up. I was desperate to be in on it. "Lieutenant," I asked. "Is there some way I could look on, here?" I waved in the direction of the camera mounted on the ceiling.

I could tell his first reaction was a flat refusal. No doubt it would be against protocol. I'd made such a mess of things earlier, why would he let me see any of this? Then I could see him reconsidering. At this point, I couldn't really still be a suspect. I'd just brought him what he must know was critical evidence. My further help clearly depended on my being familiar with what was about to happen.

"All right," he said, nodding after a moment's thought. He pointed out into the hall. "Okay, go in the next door down the hall. There's a monitor on the table in there. The speaker switch is on the wall to your right when you enter." Then he added: "Shut the door. I don't want *any* interruptions from you, Dalton. None. I'm handling this. You stay in there until I'm done and you remain quiet, okay?"

"Understood, Lieutenant. Not a peep." For a moment, Wilson looked like he was reconsidering, so I slipped out of the room before he had a chance to change his mind.

The first person who showed up appeared almost immediately after I'd closed my door in the cubicle next door and turned on the equipment. It was Senator Troy, escorted by Officer Hughes. Wilson invited Troy in and sent Hughes on his way to collect the next witness. It looked like Fitzroy and Hughes were, at least at this point, finally earning their keep.

Wilson waved the Senator to the seat at the head of the table where both of them were in full view on my screen. Troy looked around the room seeming a little bewildered—perhaps justifiably, considering the events earlier today and over the past couple of weeks.

He also, however, seemed ready to defend himself if need be. "Am I going to need a lawyer here, today, Lieutenant?" were the first words he uttered.

"Senator, I'm not going to say 'no' to that question. It's up to you, but you'll also note that I'm *not* formally warning you of your rights. I can tell you that the direction of our investigation has changed. We are recording this. I hope that's okay. With some help from you, I think we may be able to clear this up in the next couple of hours. It's your call, sir."

Troy hesitated, but then said: "All right, I'm going to take you at your word. We'll see how this goes. How does that sound?"

"Thanks, Senator. I appreciate your cooperation. Shouldn't take long, Mostly, I'd just like you to tell us if, at shortly after noon on the Monday that Senator Mortenson died, you had a conversation with Paula McPhee, the Governor's Policy Assistant for Business and Commerce."

Troy looked surprised by the question. "Uh, sure. Yeah, I did. Ran into her in the parking lot at that burger place up off the I-5 Nisqually exit. That what you're talking about?"

"It is," Wilson said. "What was said in that conversation?"

"Well, I believe we talked about the budget. She told me the Governor would consider reductions in WWRP as part of the budget deal we were working on, in exchange for some of the other requests he'd made. Damn good news, far as I was concerned."

"Anything else come up in that conversation?"

"No, not really. Not that I recall. It was just a brief interchange in the parking lot standing by her car. Not a lot of detail. Paula and I get along fine, in spite of the fact she's a Democrat. She knows I never wanted Mortenson in our Caucus. We've talked about that. But here, with the budget, was one situation where the SOB was actually doing us some good. I don't think she liked him much either, so I kidded her a little about it."

"Kidded her how?"

"I don't know. I guess I said something like: 'Maybe that jackass from Bellingham's going to be of some use after all.' She knew who I meant. We had a laugh about it. I told her I'd just left him back at his office 'working hard for the people.' Something like that."

"What happened afterward?"

"Well, I think she went inside to get something to eat."

"And you?"

"Yeah, well, what she told me actually made me change my mind about the afternoon. I'd cancelled everything and was on my way up to Seattle to visit my wife. Paula McPhee had just told me we had a shot at some scaling back in WWRP. Badly needed, in my opinion. I had a Ways & Means hearing at one thirty, and a Floor Session afterward. I decided I didn't want to be absent for that and watch them trade the WWRP concession away for something stupid. Just figured I needed to be there. So, I decided to stay. Drove back to my office instead."

"Without lunch?"

"Well, I wasn't really hungry anyway. Just feeling low. Stopped in there for some comfort food, more than anything else. That thing from the Governor's office got me going again."

"Any accidents or traffic problems on the way?

"No. Everything was fine as I recall."

"You didn't go back to your office, walk upstairs, and kill Senator Mortenson?"

Troy paused and looked across the corner of the big table. "Well, now, Lieutenant, that sounds like maybe I should have that lawyer after all." He paused. Then: "But what the hell. No, I did not do as you say. I did not kill the man. I went back and worked in my office till I went over to Ways & Means." Then Troy looked Wilson in the eye: "Exactly like I told you a week ago when you asked me that very same question."

"Thank you, Senator. You've been very helpful. With any luck, we won't need to bother you again."

I waited a moment or two for Senator Troy to leave before I went back out into the hall, but I was too quick because, when I opened my door, he was still out there adjusting his overcoat. He glanced at me in surprise. Then he glanced back in through the open conference room door and then gave me a look that was hard to interpret. It was a kind of faded smile and a shake of the head as if to say: "Good luck with *this!*" Troy probably now knew full well that I was behind the search of his office. I was hugely relieved to see that he seemed to be taking all this in stride.

When he'd gone, I stuck my head in through the conference room door. "Nicolaides here yet?" I asked Wilson.

"Not yet." Then he aimed a thumb toward the hall and, shaking his head, said: "We were definitely wrong about Troy."

"I know," I said. "I feel like a total heel."

"Finding a criminal sometimes means you've got to ask good people tough questions. Part of the job. It was your choice to…"

"…get involved. I know. I probably should have left it to you."

"You definitely should have left it to us. Nonetheless, we're headed down this road now, we're going to see where it leads. Mortenson's Assistant is on her way up, so I want you to stand by next door in case I need you." It was my signal to disappear so I went back into the adjacent room and closed the door.

Moments later, Judith Bosch and Stephanie Miles were both ushered into the conference room by Officer Fitzroy who then departed on his next "mission." Seeing Judith here, in these changed circumstances somehow made her look older. I'd always taken her for granted as Mortenson's loyal fixture of an Assistant. Here, out of that context, she looked more matronly. Stephanie, on the other hand, seemed very young and looked as if she was trying hard to fill the role of the mature, professional state legislator. Together, they appeared to be quite clearly the former teacher and student that they were.

"I gather you and Sandy Dalton had a conversation earlier, about neckties," Wilson began. Now, I'd like you to tell me as well. What color tie did the Senator usually wear?"

Bosch answered first. "Blue. Always blue. Like we told Sandy, the Senator hated red ties. He thought they made him look pasty. He was very vain about it. He thought they seemed patronizingly patriotic. All his ties were blue. Plain blue silk. He liked the feel of it. Said he could never get the knot right with a cotton tie."

Stephanie nodded. "Yeah," she said. "I don't think I ever once saw him wearing anything but blue silk. I always thought they looked, I don't know," she held up her hands and waggled her fingers. "A little too 'oh-so-classy' for a politician from a mostly rural community."

"Did he ever remove his tie when he was in the office?

"Never with visitors," Bosch replied. "Or when he went out. Always wore it. He very often took it off and put it on his credenza when he was in there working alone on something."

"On the credenza? Not on his desk."

"No. It would be in the way of his work if it was on his desk. No, folded neatly on the credenza, there along the wall. He'd keep his jacket on when he was working. The old heating system is fluky. He'd close the door to his office because he got chilly. I like a little fresh air so I like to open my window in the outer office whenever I can. He never said a word to me about it, just kept on his jacket and closed his door."

"That's all I have for right now, ladies," Wilson said. They both looked a little bewildered by the brevity of their interview as they were ushered back out of the room.

After Judith and Stephanie were gone I stayed put and watched as Wilson called reception and was, apparently, told that Aaron Nicolaides had arrived.

Moments later, Nicolaides entered, every bit the top-tier lobbyist and former House Speaker. This man was definitely wearing a silk tie. Everything about him looked expensive. Even Wilson would, no doubt, remember him from a few years back when he'd been in the news constantly. At that time, he'd tended toward jeans and a sport coat. Not anymore. I suspected that Nicolaides was not someone Wilson would be likely to take to. When they shook hands, on the screen I could almost see Wilson wince slightly at what had probably been one of Nicolaides' trademark, extra hard, "look at me, I'm a real man" handshakes.

I was glad to see that Wilson skipped some of the trivialities, even the full name and contact information. Nicolaides had laid his business card on the table. It was apparent that Wilson wanted to move things along. The moment Nicolaides was in his chair, Wilson went to the core questions: "Mr. Nicolaides, I understand you're representing Fortuna in an effort to secure some business and tax incentives for a large investment they plan to make in our state."

"That's right, Lieutenant. It's a big computer center. Several hundred million dollars involved." I was pleased to see that the answer was quick and to the point.

"You occasionally make the drive from Olympia to Seattle for meetings about that?"

"Yes. Quite frequently, actually. About that and other matters. I'm here a lot, but my office is in Seattle."

"I'm sure you've heard about the murder of Senator Abel Mortenson?"

"Of course."

"The day he died, two weeks ago today, did you make such a trip to Seattle?

"To Bellevue. Yes, I did."

"Did you have anyone with you?"

"No. Well, I'd planned to. Paula McPhee and I were supposed to have met at Nisqually for lunch, then drive up together. But, we ended up going separately."

"Did you see an accident, on your way. At Nisqually, just off the I-5 exit?"

"Yeah, that's what screwed everything up. I ended up in this long line jammed up in the right-hand lane of the freeway with all the people trying to exit. I could see the whole works ahead, the accident and everything. It's all below as you come down the grade. Nothing was moving in either direction on Martin Way. I could see that the southbound exit was all stopped too. I wasn't moving at all. I tried calling Paula, but she didn't answer. So I just decided it was silly to wait. She'd figure out, just as I did, that we'd have to change our plans. She had her car. I just went on ahead up to the Fortuna offices in Bellevue. I got there way early. Missed out on lunch. When she finally showed up, she said she'd waited for me and got caught in the traffic jam. She did make it in time anyway."

"You didn't actually get off at Nisqually?"

"Nope. Changed lanes and drove on by. Everything cleared out beyond. No problems at all."

"What kind of car do you drive, sir?"

Nicolaides looked puzzled by that, but not concerned. "It's a Town Car. Light silver. Why do you ask?"

"Can you tell me when you got there? When you arrived at the Fortuna offices?"

"Don't know exactly, but I guess it had to have been around one-fifteen, one-thirty. Something like that." Nicolaides hesitated for a moment. "This is about that Mortenson matter, right?"

"That's right."

"I see. Hmm, well, I'm not sure what you're after here, Lieutenant. I can probably pin that time down if you need me to. You fill that in on a security sheet when you check in with the Fortuna receptionist and are issued your visitor's pass. Should be a record of it."

"Okay, thanks Mr. Nicolaides," Wilson said. "I don't think we'll need that, but we'll let you know if we do. I appreciate your help."

As Nicolaides left, I saw Wilson get back on the intercom and instruct that his next witness be shown into the room.

Then he looked up at the video camera and waved at me to come in. I was thoroughly surprised by that. When he'd called reception, I'd heard him say who it was that he planned to question next. It was going to be an unusual, and potentially difficult interview. The only reason I could imagine him having for me joining him was that he hoped my presence might throw the witness off stride.

"I think you should be in here for this," he said as I came in from the hall. "Just sit over there and remain silent unless I ask you something. Understand?"

"I understand, Lieutenant," I said and took the indicated chair on the opposite side of the table, a few places down from the end.

Moments later Paula McPhee stepped in through the door. She looked irritated to be there and then very surprised to see me seated across the table. I was reasonably sure this wasn't standard practice. By having me there, Wilson was taking some kind of educated gamble. Now that she'd arrived, I very much wished I was still watching the whole thing on that monitor screen in the next room. I fervently hoped this wouldn't turn out to be another big debacle.

"Have a seat, Ms. McPhee," Wilson said, indicating the chair at the head of the table.

Paula laid her bulky handbag on the table as she sat down. It had a large, loose opening at the top and, when it tipped on its side, a couple of items slid out onto the table. She absently pushed them back inside, adjusted her position in her chair, brushed a stray hair back into place across her forehead, and then looked expectantly at Wilson, awaiting his first question.

Chapter Twenty-Seven

Monday, March 15, 3:50 p.m.

An Official Inquiry

She was lovely. Poised and confident. She noted my presence when she entered the room, but even in this rigid institutional setting, as she settled into her chair across from the alarming official presence of Lieutenant Nathan Wilson, she was composed and in control. Seeing her there, in that barren, State Patrol meeting room, reminded me how close I'd come to falling for this woman.

"Ms. McPhee, you work for the Governor's Office on Business, is that right?" Wilson asked her.

"That's correct, Lieutenant. In Business and Commerce," she said matter-of-factly.

"Is McPhee your maiden name? Or is it a married name?"

"It's the latter. My maiden name was McAllister. But I stayed with McPhee. It's my daughter's name. Both Scottish."

"Well, I've asked you here, today," Wilson continued, "for your help in our ongoing investigation into the death of Senator Abel Mortenson two weeks ago."

"Of course. I'm happy to help."

"Mr. Dalton, here, tells me you may have some information that could be useful for our investigation. Do you mind if I record our conversation?" Wilson indicated the small control panel on the table in front of them.

"No problem, Lieutenant. Please feel free."

"Good," Wilson said, pressing a button. I wasn't sure what that was about. I'd been under the impression that the video recorder had been operational since shortly after I'd arrived. Obviously, Wilson wasn't above a bit of subtle mind-play.

"Again, for the record, your name is Paula McPhee. You advise the Governor on Business and Commerce. Have I got that right?"

"Yes, you do. Perfect."

"Ms. McPhee, I want to thank you for your cooperation by speaking with me today. I'm aware you're a busy woman. I appreciate your consent to being interviewed on short notice like this."

"Of course, Lieutenant. It's no problem at all."

Wilson had just neatly secured her acknowledgment that her presence here was completely voluntary. I wondered if he'd forgo the Miranda warnings and try to rely on this being a non-custodial interview. But, no, he was a man who played safely as well as by the book. Or, perhaps, he wanted to get it out of the way early.

"Ms. McPhee, I do need to get through the formality of warning you of your rights." He took out a printed sheet and read the Miranda rights from it aloud. She gave no hint of what she might be feeling; beneath her calm she had to be in turmoil. When she agreed to waive her rights and go ahead with the interview, he slid the sheet and a pen over and asked if she'd sign at the bottom of the page. When she handed the signed form back, he slipped it into a file folder and set it carefully aside.

I didn't think Paula had ever practiced criminal law. Certainly, though, she'd remember enough from law school to appreciate the significance of that waiver. What she might not appreciate was the subtle tactic Wilson had just employed.

Over the four years I'd put in prosecuting and defending courts martial in Navy JAG, I'd seen a good many interrogation videos in which Naval Investigative Service agents had used exactly this technique. By securing a signature on a waiver of rights form and then setting the signed form aside and out of the way (the NISO guys used to slip it in a desk drawer) the interrogator created the subtle suggestion that once those rights were signed away, the witness was committed and the waiver was final. That was, of course, not the case. One could change their mind about that waiver at any time, signed or not. Paula no doubt remembered enough from law school to know that. She didn't hesitate, however. She was apparently in this whatever came.

Wilson started gently by securing some personal contact information. Then: "I take it you're the Governor's lead in securing passage of legislation that would help the Fortuna Corporation with its planned investment in a large 'computer farm' here in Washington, is that right?"

"Yes, it is. I'm working directly with Fortuna on that."

"How's that coming?"

Paula nodded, looking satisfied. "It looks good. At this point we think we're going to get enough through this Session that Fortuna will decide to go ahead with the project."

"If Senator Mortenson hadn't died two weeks ago, where do you think you'd be on that today?" said Wilson.

Paula's look of satisfaction evaporated. "Hard to say…" she began, then corrected course. "It's pretty clear we'd be a lot further away. A lot of the Republicans have serious misgivings. We still need the votes, of course, but the shift to Democratic control has made my job a lot easier." Paula's answers were slow and deliberate, as though she wanted to be sure they were completely accurate.

"Senator Mortenson's death pushed things along?"

Paula smiled. "Not like you're implying, Lieutenant. We'll get the job done. If not this year, then we'll try again next year."

"That'd be a setback for the Governor, though?"

"Yes, it would."

"And for Fortuna."

"Of course. But, come on, Lieutenant, I hope you're not suggesting somebody in the Governor's office or on the Fortuna team would have killed a Washington State Senator to help our bills pass. That's absurd. That logic could apply to half the population of the State of Washington." She looked at him dubiously. "Surely you realize that."

"I do. Of course, you're right. But, you do have something more at stake here than just another success to claim on your resume, right.?"

With that, just for an instant, Paula's self-control cracked. With a millisecond-long, angry glance in my direction she conveyed to me that she now knew exactly why I was here. She had a good idea what I'd probably told Wilson.

She was otherwise entirely composed. "Yes. I do, Lieutenant. There's the possibility of a job for me with the Morganthau Law Firm in Seattle. They will certainly be pleased if we can pass the Fortuna Package. If I miss out on a job offer, however, that isn't a motive for murder, is it? I mean, not for anybody I know, anyway." I was the target of another brief, dark, glance.

At that point, I knew my relationship with Paula was over, forever. The reality of that hit home as I watched Wilson press relentlessly forward with his questioning.

"Maybe," said Wilson. "Maybe not. Would you like to tell me where you were between noon and about one thirty on the day the Senator died."

"I was on the road headed for Bellevue."

"For a meeting at Fortuna?"

"That's right."

"I gather you stopped off on the way, at Nisqually, to buy lunch."

"Yes. At Norma's Burgers."

"When were you there?"

Paula paused for a moment. "I believe I arrived there at around quarter after twelve. I waited for a colleague who never showed up. Then left sometime after one."

"And you got to your meeting at…?"

"Around two-twenty. It was a two-thirty meeting."

"So, before you left Norma's you first waited around for something like forty or fifty minutes, maybe a little more, before getting back on the road. Why was that?"

"As I said, I was waiting to meet up with a colleague."

"Aaron Nicolaides?"

Again, the glance. "Yes. Aaron and I were supposed to have met there. We were planning to get something to eat. Then I was going to leave my car and we'd drive to Seattle together in his. He was planning to return to Olympia for a legislative reception that evening."

"So, you got to Nisqually at quarter after twelve. Nisqually is, what, less than an hour to Bellevue. You waited for forty-five minutes plus and you still got to Bellevue early for your two-thirty meeting. Why did you show up at Nisqually so early? What were you planning to do with all that extra time?"

"We were going to eat lunch, Lieutenant."

"On the road? Or inside the restaurant?"

"Aaron always prefers to sit down. We had a lot to talk about and wanted some time." One of the perfect locks of dark hair beside Paula's ear looked like it had become moist and had matted down against her temple.

Paula continued: "I'm not sure I understand where you're going with all this, Lieutenant. If it's about Senator Mortenson, I wasn't even in town. I was seen at Norma's."

"Yes, you were. By Senator Troy, right?"

"That's right. And by a friend of Sandy's. Clive Curtin."

"And you and Senator Troy discussed the State Budget and the WWRP appropriation?"

"Yes, we did. He saw me there, already on my way to Bellevue."

"That's right, Ms. McPhee," Wilson confirmed. "It's just what Senator Troy said. Then, when he left, you went inside. You then came back out to wait for Nicolaides, right?"

"Right. Mostly, I sat in the car with my phone."

"He never showed up?" She just nodded at this. "Um, perhaps you could make an audible answer to that." Wilson prompted, pointing at his recorder. "For the record?"

"Yes. That's right. I went outside and waited. Aaron never came."

"That's when you saw the accident?"

"That's right," she said, eyes straight ahead, pointedly not looking at me. "When it happened, I was standing in the parking lot next to my car."

"Tell me about it."

"A big silver car, maybe a Town Car or something, came from that side road where the northbound offramp ends. Went right through a red light. A brown Corolla coming from the southbound offramp overpass swerved to miss it and hit another guy who was heading north. The silver car stopped for a second, and then took off up Martin Way headed south. I didn't see who was driving. It had tinted windows."

I was completely taken aback. She'd omitted Nicolaides entirely. This must be what she'd told Wilson's colleague earlier today when she'd followed my suggestion and called in to report what she'd seen. I realized then that everything she'd said to me about believing Nicolaides was driving that car had been a lie.

When I'd first learned from Clive that she'd stopped at Norma's that day, I'd wondered why she hadn't mentioned it or the accident last Friday evening when we'd had dinner together at the Lemon Tree. Norma's had come up at the time. Given the context of that conversation, it seemed natural that she would have mentioned it. Seeing the accident there was also an odd thing to have simply omitted.

This morning at her office, when I'd asked her about it directly, she must have realized she needed an explanation. So, she'd lied, telling me she believed the large silver car was Nicolaides' Town Car. That and the job offer would explain for me why she might not have wanted to mention it to me before—awkward, but still a much better explanation than the truth. It also explained why she hadn't reported seeing the accident to the police.

Now she was faced with a different problem. She needed to explain that supposed forty-five or fifty-minute wait at Norma's. It was obvious she could have left at any time given that the southbound lanes on Martin Way were clear. The only explanation she had was that she'd been waiting for Arron Nicolaides. Unfortunately, that wouldn't make sense if she'd actually believed Nicolaides was the driver of that hit-and-run car. If she'd believed that, she'd have left right then, not waited around for someone who clearly wasn't coming.

The part of her story about believing it had been Nicolaides had now evaporated.

At that point, I sensed a change in Paula's demeanor. She was starting to look defensive. Even defiant. I had the feeling she might be about to demand that the questioning stop and that she see an attorney.

I think Wilson sensed the same thing. He did something I'm sure is totally contrary to police procedure; something that constituted a big risk for him. It definitely caught *me* by surprise.

I'd guess it caught Paula off guard as well.

Instead of pressing forward with his interrogation, Wilson turned to me, and said: "So, Mr. Dalton. I believe you've discovered a few items of interest over the past couple of hours or so. Would you like to ask a question or two?" I looked across the table at him and was startled to realize that this situation was precisely why he'd invited me to join him in this interview.

Just like that, I found myself in the hot seat. One I'd made for myself.

Chapter Twenty-Eight

Monday, March 15, 4:10 p.m.

Suspension of the Rules

Looking back, it is difficult to admit, even to myself, that I did what followed. I suppose once my instincts as a lawyer took over, there was no going back.

"Your ex-husband, his name is Douglas? Douglas Frederick McPhee?" I asked.

She looked startled by the change of direction. Surprised that I knew his name. She knew she'd never mentioned it to me. "Uh huh, that's right, Sandy. He goes by Doug."

"Mr. McPhee is in the yacht repair and delivery business, am I right?"

"Yes," she said, looking worried.

"He has a website: 'McPhee Yacht Service and Delivery?' It's located in Seattle?"

"Yes. That's him."

"I take it he's often off sailing in various quarters of the planet. Can't very well take care of a daughter. So that's how you ended up with Marissa?"

"More or less."

"And that's been the situation for the past ten years or so?"

"Yes."

"Paula, you're not actually divorced from Mr. McPhee, are you? The two of you are still married as of today?"

Paula was visibly disturbed by my questions. I doubt she'd been expecting any of this to come up. "Yes, Sandy," she said. This time her voice had softened. "I know I should have said something…"

"Does he ever spend time with your daughter?" I interrupted. "Visitation or something?"

"No. I never see him. Neither does she. I don't think Marissa would know him if she saw him." The late sun had broken through the clouds and was beating in through the outside window. It cast a bright light onto the conference table and across the chair in which Paula sat. She shifted position to avoid squinting into the sun as she spoke. The defiance I'd seen a few moments ago had vanished.

"Does Doug provide support?" I continued.

"No."

"Yet you've made no effort to take the man to court for child support or to divorce him for over a decade. Why? Why have you spent ten years married to a man who provides no support, who you don't care for and never see?"

She didn't answer. She just sat there looking stricken.

At this point, Officer Fitzroy opened the conference room door and looked inside. Wilson waved him in and the two of them stepped down to the end of the room and conversed quietly for a few moments. Fitzroy handed Wilson a thin file folder and a bulky envelope. As Paula and I waited, dust mites hung suspended in the silence of the room, illuminated by the sun's rays.

Then Fitzroy left the room and Wilson returned to his seat, waiving at me to continue.

Paula's eyes turned to me. Pleading for help. No longer was she the strong, confident woman I knew. The bright blue scarf around her neck had come slightly askew. I was causing pain, irreversible pain. My own emotions were a jumble over what I'd learned in the past few hours. Over the lies I'd been told. Over what I knew she'd done. At the same time, also over my continued feelings for her. I was on a tightrope. I wanted to help, but I could not.

I would not.

Instead, I pushed on: "You have a problem, don't you Paula? You and Doug had taken on the care and upbringing of a Native American child, a child who would be eligible for membership in the Swinomish Indian Tribe… if they knew about her?"

Again, Paula didn't answer.

"But they don't, do they? The Swinomish Indian Tribe doesn't know anything about Marissa?"

"No," she said quietly. "I don't believe they do."

"Because you never actually completed a formal adoption, did you? You and your husband, Doug?" I knew this because it was the other thing absent from the records at the Thurston County Courthouse and online at Skagit County and King County. No divorce, and no adoption. Both of them had been living in Seattle at the time they'd taken on Marissa's care. Doug still resided there. She had later become and now remained a resident of Thurston County.

"No," she said, looking defeated and miserable. "Marissa's mom, Shana, needed my help. We were friends in high school. Shana's Swinomish but, by the time I got out of law school and had started working she was living in Seattle, trying to get away from her parents and from the reservation. She'd gotten into drugs and was living on the street. She asked for my help—asked me to look after Marissa while she got cleaned up and pulled her act together. She wanted her daughter to grow up and make a life for herself off-reservation. She couldn't manage that on her own as a single mom with a high school education. Marissa needed a home so we took her in. After that, Shana disappeared and never came back. We couldn't find her. It wasn't until more than a year later that we learned she'd died. By then…"

What both Paula and I knew, and I'm sure Wilson knew as well, is that there is a Federal statute, the Indian Child Welfare Act adopted back in 1978. It gives special authority to Indian Tribes over custody, care, and adoption of Native American children under eighteen years of age. If the courts or tribal authorities learned about Marissa and knew she was being raised without formal custody by a non-Indian, there was and had been from the start, every probability Paula could lose her daughter. I'd looked it up. Paula's distant Swinomish blood wouldn't carry much weight with the Tribe. Her lack of cultural connections to the tribe would count heavily against her. After all this time, they'd also be very angry with her for failing to connect Marissa with her cultural roots

"If you divorced him, you know your 'custody' of Marissa could become an issue?"

"Yes," she said softly.

"Why hasn't Douglas divorced *you*?" I asked.

Paula sighed. "He's happy the way things are." Her voice was so soft

I had to lean in to hear her. "He's off delivering boats most of the time. He has a running string of girlfriends and no desire to settle down. For ten years, I've been worried he'd find someone he cared about and want to finally remarry. It's never happened. At least not yet. I think Doug, in his own way, cares about Marissa too. He never visits. But he doesn't especially want to see her get caught up in a legal custody mess, or put out to foster care."

"In just a few more years, what, five or six, Marissa will come of age and the whole thing will become irrelevant?"

"That's right. I wanted to bide my time."

"Something changed, though, didn't it Paula? Something happened to make you need to take action."

"No," she said firmly but softly.

It was a lie and she knew I knew it. I waited a moment, allowing a noisy motorcycle to pass by outside. Then I continued, ignoring her answer: "Were you worried about being discovered? Had Doug said something? What was it? What happened?"

She shook her head, but then: "Marissa was asking questions," she said, surrendering.

"Questions?"

"She came home from school one day. She asked me... wanted to know if I was her mother. I... I didn't know how to answer her." She paused to collect herself. "I never had much contact with my Swinomish heritage. I wanted that for her. Wanted her to have some connection to her roots. I was afraid. It had all just gone on too long. Never knowing where we stood with Doug. And..."

"And?"

With this, Paula McPhee, was near to tears, looking pathetic, defensive, and incredibly beautiful all at the same time. She looked across that table at me with those deep, irresistible, dark eyes in a way that, two hours earlier, would have made my knees buckle.

"And... I was falling for you, Sandy," she said. "I thought we had a chance together. I wanted to see if I could make it work between us."

I'll admit, hearing her say that shook me. I'd been half-way in love with her for a couple of months now. Whenever I'd moved closer, she would close down. Initially I'd just chocked it up to lack of interest. Or, I thought maybe she wanted to focus on her professional ambitions. Now I understood.

After reading that CSI report earlier this afternoon, however, remembering the blue silk ties I believed Mortenson had worn, and recalling my own red cotton tie, I'd started to wonder. That was, initially, why I'd made that run over to the Thurston County Courthouse and had checked out the Skagit and King County records as well. Until then, I hadn't given Marissa's Tribal connection much thought. Then I'd also looked up the registration rules on the Swinomish website. That was where Paula's secrets had finally been revealed.

At every point along the way, Paula had done or tried to do the right thing. Her friend Shana had needed help. Marissa had needed a home. Once Paula learned that Shana was gone for good, she'd been caring for Marissa for over a year. How could she have then torn this vulnerable three-year-old's life apart once again just to see her end up in foster care? For ten years she'd held off seeking a divorce, putting her own life on hold for the sake of her daughter.

Now, with Paula looking at me in desperation, a part of me wanted to call off all the questioning, to go over, take her in my arms, and lead her out of this ugly, echoing institutional room and carry her to safety.

I knew it couldn't happen. It was too late for her—too late for me as well.

"You also wanted to solidify your custody of Marissa, right?" I said softly. "You wanted to be absolutely sure Douglas was well and truly cut off from the 'daughter' he hardly knew?"

"Yes, that too."

"So, you approached Douglas about it. You asked him for a divorce, one that would be agreed to between the two of you. No mention would be made of Marissa at all. It would just be a no-contest, mutually agreed dissolution of the marriage. No particular property settlement. No fuss. Just signed by a Court Commissioner, filed, and forgotten. Right."

"That's right. We could have left Marissa out of it." She said.

"So, what went wrong?"

She shifted in her seat. This was the question she'd known was coming. The one she'd been avoiding from the start. I was acutely aware of Lieutenant Wilson's presence in the room, across the table to Paula's left. He'd pushed his chair back and was out of Paula's line of sight, but she obviously knew he was there. Knew every word she spoke was being recorded. Must have known that the outcome, here, was now inevitable. It seemed as though she was captured by my questions and maybe by me. It was as if, at this point, the two of us were alone, talking privately here together in this room without the entire police power of the State of Washington watching over our shoulders.

"Doug refused," she said in a final, futile gesture of defiance.

If Doug had refused, Mortenson would never have become involved. She'd have had no motive to kill him. "Come on, Paula," I insisted gently. "You know what he's going to say when he's asked. He didn't refuse at all, did he? He was perfectly willing, wasn't he?"

Again she didn't answer.

"But he told his father what you wanted," I said.

That was the point at which Paula McPhee began to cry. I had never seen her cry. Maybe her tears were artifice, I don't know. They didn't seem that way to me. I couldn't help being deeply affected. Still, I knew exactly what she'd done. With that last question, she knew I knew. That meant she knew the Lieutenant also knew.

With those tears, Paula's world was disintegrating. The life she had worked for years to assemble was collapsing around her. She'd had everything at stake here. Her career. Her hopes for the future. Her beloved daughter and her daughter's future. Perhaps even me. It was all in rubble, and I was the cause, or at least the cause of making it known.

She sobbed for a few moments, and then pulled herself together, looked across the table at me with profound disappointment. Drawing upon a faint remnant of recovered integrity, she said:

"Yes, he told his father."

I'd done some creative guessing in the past couple of hours. It had started with a long, careful look at the pictures of the owner posted on the website of Douglas McPhee's boat service and delivery firm, home-ported in Seattle's Ballard district. I knew that face. Then I'd recalled what I'd been told two weeks earlier by former schoolteacher Judith Bosch, about how she'd counseled a certain troubled tenth-grader from a broken home who hated school but loved boats. I recalled the man who had stood beside the widow at that memorial service in Bellingham a couple of Saturdays ago. What I'd realized was that Paula's husband, Douglas Frederick McPhee, was none other than Senator Abel Mortenson's troubled son, Dougie. Dougie, whose custody had gone to his mother and who had then inherited his mother's maiden name, McPhee. He'd passed that name along to Paula through their failed marriage, and also to Marissa.

Despite the loss of custody, Dougie's divorced father, back when Dougie was at Seaholm High School in Bellingham, had been involved enough with the boy's life to have come to the school for a parent-teacher conference with Judith Bosch. That father-son connection had continued right up until the moment of the Senator's death.

Mortenson knew about Marissa, of course. He'd kept silent all these years, perhaps out of a wish to let his son live his own life. Perhaps, also because he knew his son's participation in Marissa's care without reporting it could potentially have exposed him to charges of child abduction—charges to which Paula was also exposed.

After all these years, Douglas was probably, finally, washed clean by time. By statute of limitations, most felonies couldn't be prosecuted after five or six years had passed. Mortenson also knew, however, that petitions for divorce in every county required the completion of a detailed questionnaire. It would include questions about dependent children. If Dougie agreed to a consent divorce and signed such a questionnaire without truthfully revealing the continuing illegal custody of Marissa, he might well be making a false or misleading statement concealing his original wrongdoing and also becoming an accessory to Paula's ongoing crime. This could potentially renew his criminal exposure for child abduction and also open him up to prosecution for perjury.

Abel Mortenson wasn't going to let that happen. He probably blamed Paula for his son's failed marriage. He decided to report Paula's custody of Marissa to the Swinomish Tribe before Dougie and Paula went ahead with their divorce. There was very little doubt that he would have told his son, warning him not to sign those papers. Dougie had, no doubt, then told Paula.

"Paula," I said. "I'm betting that envelope, over there, the thick one that Lieutenant Wilson was given, a few minutes ago, contains a certain red, cotton necktie. My necktie, as it happens. The one I recall having removed and given to you when we went to the beach with Marissa on Sunday afternoon after the wedding, the afternoon before Abel Mortenson's death. I believe you put it in your bag. You wouldn't have noticed, but that tie has a small black mark on the label that I was able to identify when I saw it here at the State Patrol Office earlier today. That necktie was found at the scene of Senator Mortenson's murder. It was covered in blood, his blood. It had been used to wipe off the Lummi hunting knife that was used in his murder."

Paula just stared at me, overwhelmed by sadness.

"Here's what I think happened," I said. "I think when Doug told you that his father was going to report Marissa to the Swinomish Tribe, you became frantic. He probably called you the very morning of the day Mortenson died. I'm sure you know that some of the Morganthau firm's clients are Indian Tribes who would not take lightly the discovery that the firm that represented them was hiring a lawyer who had been illegally raising a Native American child. Maybe that had something to do with what you did. I don't know. But, far more important than anything else was that you knew if you didn't do something you could lose Marissa. You knew your own faint blood relationship to the Swinomish Tribe would mean nothing to them. Your lack of cultural connection would also be damming. Marissa is a full-blooded Swinomish—even if she was born off reservation and has never registered officially with the Tribe.

"You had to act.

"You had a full schedule that day including a meeting at Fortuna at two-thirty that afternoon, and a drive there with Aaron Nicolaides whom, as you said, you'd arranged to meet at Norma's at about twelve-twenty. As you got out of your car at Norma's, you ran into Senator Troy. You decided to mention the Governor's WWRP concession and the two of you had a brief conversation. He mentioned that he'd just seen Senator Mortenson at his office and you knew he'd be there working in that mostly-empty building, as he often did, over the lunch hour, alone with his door closed.

"You went inside Norma's and then came back out to wait. You were standing there in the lot, waiting for Aaron to arrive, and watching the cars come down the Northbound off ramp, around the corner, and through that intersection. All the while you were, no doubt, seething with anxiety, painfully aware that, at that very moment, Mortenson could be picking up his phone and punching in that fateful call.

"When the accident happened, you saw the whole thing. You saw the aftermath, the huge traffic snarl that inevitably resulted from a near fatality accident at a major interchange. All the cars going on or coming off the freeway at Nisqually, headed in either direction, have to go through that same light. It's a busy place. Almost immediately, the traffic backed up. The northbound cars taking that exit were backed all the way up the ramp and onto the freeway. From where you stood, you could see it all. Nothing was moving. It wasn't going to be moving for some time to come.

"You knew Aaron would be caught in that traffic. Everything on Martin Way headed toward that intersection and toward Norma's was blocked as well. There was no way the two of you were going to meet there that day, have lunch, and still make your two-thirty in Bellevue. That was obvious immediately.

"You probably considered calling him. But, you changed your mind as you realized that the entire situation gave you a perfect opportunity, what might be your only opportunity. The southbound lanes on Martin Way, the ones headed away from the accident, were open. You knew you had plenty of time to drive back to Olympia, park in your assigned space right on Campus, confront your husband's father, and still easily get back on the road and make your meeting in Bellevue. If you were late for the meeting, you could just complain about how you had been snarled up in the traffic mess caused by the accident.

"Whatever your plan, when you saw Mortenson in his office, all smug and powerful, fully prepared to ruin your life and your daughter's, and when he remained determined to report you and Marissa, you were frightened and angry. You saw that ceremonial Lummi Indian knife displayed there so proudly on his desk and it reminded you of everything you stood to lose. The man's hypocrisy and hatefulness seemed boundless. That knife was also a symbol of everything you hated about him.

"You dropped your handbag on his big desk, took that knife, and killed him with it.

"In the process, just as happened right here at this table when you arrived a few minutes ago when you laid down your handbag, it came open and some of its contents spilled out onto Senator Mortenson's desk. Probably, one of those items was the necktie I'd given you on Sunday afternoon and which you'd put in your purse where both of us forgot all about it. After our dinner last Friday evening, when we parted there on the sidewalk out in front of my office, you actually dug around in your bag a moment, looking for it, thinking this would be a chance to return it to me.

"Then you remembered: it wasn't there. And why.

"Somehow, in Mortenson's office my tie may even have gotten blood on it. Maybe the Senator grabbed it with his own bloody hands in the final struggle. Maybe there was some splatter. There was also blood on your hands. Maybe even some on your clothing.

"Of course, your fingerprints were on the handle of that knife.

"You grabbed my cotton tie, which may or may not have already been bloody, and used it to wipe off the knife handle. Then you didn't want to put the messy thing back in your purse, did you? You'd get blood all over everything else in your bag. It was also incriminating; you didn't want that bloody tie in your possession at all. You noted that the Senator wasn't wearing a tie so you decided just to leave my tie there on his desk to be taken for his. Then, glancing around, you saw his tie laying on the credenza. A nice clean blue silk tie. You stuffed that into your purse and took it with you, leaving mine behind.

"Then you left the building, perhaps planning to somehow mask your appearance in the security camera. Until you saw, or maybe you already knew, since you are in and out of that building all the time, that the camera had been sprayed with black paint by some vandal. And you knew you were home free. The lunch hour hallway was empty. You slipped down the back stairs and out the back door without ever being seen.

"When you got to your car, you still had well over an hour remaining to make your two-thirty meeting. Your home is only a few blocks away. Even if you had to stop by there to change clothes, you had lots of time. When you got to Bellevue, you made sure to commiserate with Aaron Nicolaides about the horrible traffic jam you'd both experienced at Nisqually."

Feeling breathless after my lengthy diatribe, I waited a moment or two, and glanced at the Lieutenant. He seemed fine with how everything was going and gave me a little nod as if to say: "Go ahead and finish it."

So, I did.

"Paula, that thin little file right over there, the other one Lieutenant Wilson was given by his associate a few minutes ago, I'm sure what that one contains is a copy of the search warrant for your apartment, for your car, for your office in the Insurance Building, and for your personal belongings." Both she and I glanced at Wilson who nodded his head. "You might want to think about the State Patrol officers who are, at this very moment, executing that warrant. Think hard about what they're likely to find. Among other things, I'd say it's a reasonable bet they may find some blood-stained clothing. Perhaps even a certain blue silk necktie that is an exact match to ones belonging to Senator Mortenson, maybe that even has some of Mortenson's trace DNA. They may even find some of Mortenson's microscopic blood splatter on it; some you failed to see."

While I'd been questioning her, and without my noticing, Lieutenant Wilson's officers, the faithful Fitzroy and Hughes, had slipped back into the room and taken up a position just inside the door. Now Fitzroy quietly moved over and stood against the wall a step or two behind Paula's chair.

I continued: "I think it might be interesting to look inside your handbag right now." I nodded at her large stylish bag laying in front of her on the conference room table and glanced at Wilson who nodded back. The handbag would be included in the warrant. Probably there would be nothing of importance in that bag. I knew Paula well enough to know she tended to collect things there and then forget about them. It just seemed worth a try.

She made a motion, perhaps to pick it up and hand it over, perhaps not, but Fitzroy got there first, sliding her bag across the table toward Lieutenant Wilson.

Before picking it up, Wilson, slowly and methodically, opened his notebook and wrote something at the top of a blank page, presumably a list for future reference of what we were about to find. Without rising from his seat, Wilson drew a copy of the warrant out of the file and slid it across the table to Paula. Then he reached out and upended the bag. The contents tumbled out onto the table. A few of the smaller items slid a foot or two across the slick laminate surface. A lipstick container rolled all the way across in my direction making a sharp, echoing "tick, tick, tick" in the otherwise totally silent room. I caught it before it went on the floor.

Everything else landed in a compact heap.

In the center of that heap was a shiny blue silk men's necktie.

Chapter Twenty-Nine

Tuesday, March 16, 9:45 a.m.

Sine Die

I t was a calm, clear, morning as I hurried across campus to attend the second and final hearing on Capitol security in the Senate Committee on Law and Justice.

Up on the Capitol steps, a group of activist organizers was setting up signs, testing a sound system, greeting new arrivals, speaking together with arms pointing this way and that as they orchestrated a protest on some issue planned for later in the day. On the opposite side of the Capitol Building, the usual knot of lobbyists and nervous constituents had gathered by the sundial, arguing strategies, telling tales, striking deals, congratulating, and commiserating. The occasional legislator hurried past, into and out of the office buildings on their way to an important meeting or, perhaps, to cast a critical vote.

The first-floor hallway of the Cherberg Building was busy, as usual. In a few minutes, Senator Arlo Devine would reconvene his Law and Justice Committee on its pioneering investigative mission to keep the Capitol safe and the government functioning. His was but one of several hearings scheduled here this morning. A few of the hard-core reporters were back, but most of those in the hallway this morning were here on other business.

An arrest had been reported in last night's late news. It had taken two weeks. But, this morning, just sixteen hours later, the Legislature was already moving on.

As I made my way through the knots of people in the hall, Senator Digger Troy was just behind. I held the hearing room door open for him, a gesture he acknowledged with a brief smile.

I'd stopped by his office in the Newhouse Building first thing this morning to apologize as abjectly as I knew how. Thankfully, he'd been philosophical even if his Legislative Assistant, judging by her venomous look, still bore a serious grudge. He told me he hadn't been all that troubled by the search. He'd disliked Abel Mortenson, but he'd also known there was nothing incriminating to be found. Even so, I knew I'd added to the burdens he'd suffered in recent months. It wasn't something of which I was proud.

Troy had told me he'd talked with his son by phone last night and had decided not to run for re-election. He'd finish out his current term, but then he'd be returning, full time, to ranching. He looked sad but functional as he took an empty chair near the back of Hearing Room Two and awaited the commencement of proceedings. After the Session adjourned in another month or so, he'd be back atop a horse, riding fences, and running cattle in the eastern foothills of the Cascades.

He looked sad but, on balance, what I read in him was mostly relief.

Jerry Stockmeyer got to the hearing room just as Senator Devine was bringing the gavel down. He was with another Northwest Tribal Fisheries Consortium staffer, someone I didn't know. He waved, but the two of them found a seat together on the other side of the room.

Last night, it had been nearly eight before they'd been done with me at the State Patrol office, so I'd decided to spend the night in Olympia. On my walk back to the office I'd called Jerry at home and we'd had a nice conversation.

Apparently, yesterday had been Jerry's birthday. The big "four oh." He'd been giving a lot of thought to where his life was headed. Even his treasured work at the NTFC was beginning to feel futile and unappreciated. He'd told me he'd been quite depressed as he'd gone into to the office yesterday morning.

Over lunch, however, Jerry's colleagues at NTFC had thrown him a little birthday party. There was a cake, candles, soft drinks, a card, some speeches and gentle roasting. The whole bit.

Some of the NTFC Board Members had been there. One, a deeply-respected former Chief of one of their member tribes, had made a little speech, kidding around about Jerry's foibles and thanking him for his commitment to the NTFC cause. Then he'd revealed something that came to Jerry as a huge surprise and embarrassment.

Apparently, from the day of that hearing, last Session, when the sportsmen had come in and killed my "catch the full non-Tribal 50% share" bill, there had been rampant speculation within the NTFC over who had tipped them off. Jerry was the prime suspect. Who else knew enough of the details? Who else knew who to tell? Who else but Jerry would be likely to take it personally enough, and think it through enough, to actually go ahead with it? Jerry's obvious discomfort whenever the matter came up had apparently been the final tell. Over the past year, some of his colleagues had even needled him about it a few times, but he'd never caught on. So, it had become something of a fondly held secret around the office. It had, after all, turned out well. Nobody outside the NTFC had a clue who'd done it.

When the Chief had made that all known, there'd been a chorus of friendly laughter and slaps on the back from Jerry's bosses and co-workers. It turned out that all of them saw Jerry's "guilty" act as further proof of his absolute commitment to his work and of his steadfast loyalty to his grateful employers.

I was surprised to see House Speaker Jackson Thiel attending the hearing. Representative Stephanie Miles showed up as well—if a little late. She looked particularly pleased with herself as she made her way up the aisle to take a vacant seat beside Thiel near the front of the room. They nodded to each other in a way that suggested they'd arranged to meet and were planning to talk together when the hearing was over.

I had a fairly good idea what they might discuss.

Earlier this morning, I'd caught a thread in the news for a report from the *Bellingham Herald*. A prominent private Bellingham law firm had announced that George Turner, the current Whatcom County Executive, was about to join the firm. There was strong speculation that he'd be stepping down as County Executive at the end of his current term. Without him running for re-election, it seemed almost certain that Phil Sheridan, the County's extremely popular Assessor, would drop his bid for Mortenson's Senate seat even though he looked to be a slam dunk with the County Council. Instead, Sheridan would almost certainly decide to run for County Executive, a full-time paid position with a lot of power, prestige, no commute to Olympia, and a terrific platform for higher office. With passage of Steph's public farmland bill, she was gaining useful popular support in the local food community, an increasingly active constituency. So, with Sheridan out of the running, it was my bet Stephanie Miles would be next in line to take his place in filling Mortenson's now-vacant seat in the Senate. That meant Thiel and the Democrats would need to be thinking about who might be taking Stephanie's place in the House.

At one point, as the Chair called up a new witness, Stephanie turned around, caught my eye, and gave me a big smile. I could almost see the gears working. I knew rumors were flying about my connection to Paula McPhee's arrest, and about our relationship. Now, I'd be "available." I fully expected to face yet another "introduction" to some eligible female before the week was out, thanks to Stephanie's desire to be a matchmaker.

Lieutenant Wilson was up front testifying about last night's arrest by the time Martin Rose slipped into the hearing room maybe five minutes late. Martin gave me a nod, and sat in the back. I'd run into Martin earlier today while grabbing some early coffee over in the Prichard Building. When I'd sat down across the table from him, he'd had a strange look on his face. Clearly something was up. "Okay," I'd said. "What's on your mind? You're obviously dying to tell me something."

"I am," he'd said, looking very somber.

"Come on. Spill it," I said, preparing myself to hear some bad news.

"Well, Sandy, I'm afraid you're going to have to get used to dealing with a new Legislative Liaison at Fish and Wildlife."

That didn't sound good. "Come on. You're leaving?"

"I'm afraid I am."

Had his concerns about fallout from his senseless mistake while testifying before House Natural Resources earlier this Session finally been realized? "You can't mean…"

"Yep. After today, I'm afraid I'll no longer be working for David Prince."

I'd had nothing to say to that. It blew me away, even if, perhaps I could have seen it coming.

I'd already been formulating what to say in commiseration, when he'd suddenly broken into an incredible grin. "It turns out," he'd said, "Governor Browne wants me to step in to replace Lawrence Peoples as his Director of Legislative Affairs."

That took me by surprise. "What? Now you *are* kidding."

"Nope. It's True. I start immediately. Director Prince recommended me. I'm moving into my new office this afternoon."

It was amazing news. "Really? Damn. The Governor's lobbyist. Good for you, Martin. Damn." I'd reached across and shook his hand. He was beaming.

The whole situation just tickled me. After all his worries about Tony Underhill and that damn testimony. I just couldn't help laughing. He'd been completely convinced he was about to get fired. Prince had even recommended him.

"I know, I know," Martin had said, shaking his head and smiling. "I guess there's no getting out of it now. I'm definitely going to owe my wife that crab dinner."

Shortly after Martin arrived, I saw Stephanie reach in her bag and pull out what looked like her phone. She looked down for a moment, then leaned over and excused herself with Speaker Thiel, got up, walked to the back of the room and stepped out into the hall. She left her coat and bag behind. After a few minutes' absence, she came back into the room with Judith Bosch, the two of them smiling and talking softly. Judith headed for a chair in the back, sat down, and watched the proceedings while Stephanie walked back up to the front and returned to her seat next to Thiel.

With that, another piece also fell into place. If Stephanie Miles was about to move over to the Senate, she was going to need a Legislative Assistant. I knew she wasn't especially happy with the one she currently employed—an ambitious young man who'd just graduated in Political Science from Western Washington University and was more interesting in building his own political network than in helping her keep her appointments organized. There was no way she'd want to take him with her when she moved over to the Senate.

Judith was another matter entirely. Her present employment with Senate Natural Resources Committee would certainly come to an end when this Session adjourned. She would, no doubt, be out on the job market, an older woman with a resume that might not mean much to a lot of employers. Judith had been working for Abel Mortenson for years. She knew the processes, the politics, and the people both in the Legislature and in the 42nd District. When Stephanie made that move, I had no doubt at all that Judith would be with her—once again serving as the Legislative Assistant to the Senator from the 42nd District. This time, she'd be working for a close friend as well as, finally, for someone she, no doubt, considered a real Democrat.

I was happy for Judith for another reason as well. With the 'Ds' in charge, the higher WWRP appropriation was now in the bag. It looked like her dad would be able to protect his family farm and finally retire.

One person I didn't see at the hearing was Clive Curtin. I had, however, noticed in this morning's news that a settlement had finally been reached between the State and the Tribes that would allow the normal fishing season to proceed as usual this summer. They'd obviously managed to reach agreement without any help from us. Not that I'd ever had any clear idea how we might have helped.

I'd been told that Clive owned a home on Bainbridge Island, a thirty-five-minute ferry ride across Puget Sound from downtown Seattle. At one occasion last year, in a moment of pointless curiosity, I'd actually looked him up on the website of the Kitsap County Assessor and had found the address. His home was on waterfront property on Port Blakely along the east side of Bainbridge looking across the Sound toward the Seattle skyline. According to online retail websites, the place was worth a couple of million dollars. Some photos showed a boathouse at the top of the beach, some kind of launching ramp, and a nice, twenty-five-or-so-foot Trophy sport fishing boat moored at an anchor buoy in the bay just out front.

With announcement of the settlement, I was willing to bet that Clive and his friends were already looking forward to their summer plans on the water. With today's clear weather, maybe Curtin had taken some time off to work on his boat in preparation for the coming summer. But then, as I gave that some further thought, I realized that even if he wasn't hard at work in his impressive office high in the Columbia Center, it was more likely he'd be out organizing signature-gatherers in his seemingly tireless effort to put my clients out of business.

The current Legislative sport priority bill might be dead. But I would, doubtless, still have my fill of Clive Curtin over the course of the coming months. It wouldn't be a good idea for me to ever lose sight of that reality.

The night before, at Patrol Headquarters just before Wilson and I parted, Wilson had gone so far as to thank me for my help on the case. I'd had a brief moment to savor that, and to feel like I might have actually been useful. Then he added: "For a while there, I have to admit I was starting to think it all might just be too complicated to figure out." He gave a little shrug. "In the end," he concluded, "it had nothing to do with politics. It was all just a family matter."

He was right, of course. If it hadn't been so personal for me, he wouldn't have needed my help at all.

Looking back on the final interrogation in the State Patrol office, I knew that to Paula I must have seemed brutally vengeful. In reality, with every question she'd been asked, first by Wilson, then by me, I'd been hoping, half-expecting even, that she'd answer in some way that would prove me wrong. Instead, her guilt had become clearer with every word she'd spoken.

Even as Fitzroy and Hughes had finally led her away I'd been staggered to realize just how much I still cared.

"I'm sorry Paula," was all I'd had to say.

She'd said nothing in reply.

The balance of the Law and Justice hearing passed in a blur. When the Chair finally gaveled it to a close, the room was nearly empty. It appeared that the total legislative response to Abel Mortenson's murder would turn out to be a new budget line-item of $50,000 reallocated from other critical State appropriations and devoted instead to replacing and maintaining security cameras at the Washington State Capitol.

The Senator was a man whose life's work had been measured in trade-offs. So too, it seemed, would be his legacy.

About The Author

Don Stuart has over 20 years of lobbying experience in the Washington, Oregon, and Idaho State Legislatures and in the U.S. Congress. He served as Executive Director for Salmon for Washington, a trade group representing commercial fishermen and fish processing firms (1990-96), Executive Director for the Washington Association of Conservation Districts, a professional association representing local governments assisting agricultural landowners (1997-2000), and Northwest Regional Director for American Farmland Trust, a national environmental organization protecting local farmland from development (2000-2011). Don was also the campaign manager and public spokesperson in the successful defense of a Washington statewide anti-commercial fishing ballot initiative (I-640) in 1995 and he ran for the U.S. Congress in Washington's First District in 1996.

Don is also a former Alaska commercial salmon troll fisherman (1962-65, 1980-89), a formerly practicing Seattle trial attorney (1972-79), and was a Lieutenant in the U.S. Navy Judge Advocate General's Corps during the Viet Nam War (1968-72). His opinion column on fish politics appeared monthly in the Fishermen's News from 1990-96. He is the author of *Barnyards and Birkenstocks: Why Farmers and Environmentalists Need Each Other*, published by Washington State University Press (2014), and of *The Washington Guide to Small Claims Court*, published by Self-Counsel Press (1979).

CPSIA information can be obtained
at www.ICGtesting.com
Printed in the USA
FSOW01n1230221117
41449FS